# Murder for Me

# Murder for Me

Russell Little

ISBN-13: 9780692722183
ISBN-10: 0692722181
Library of Congress Control Number: 2016901959
Russell Little Press

*This book is dedicated to my mother who helped foster in me a love of reading and encouraged my story telling. I miss you.*

# ACKNOWLEDGEMENT

I want to thank Cathy Spies, who graciously volunteered to edit my book when I was getting started. I am humbled by her support, encouragement and time. Without her, I would never have completed my first novel. I also want to thank my writers' group who helped me tremendously by pointing out inconsistencies and helping me to stay on track. Thank you especially to Eric Thuesen, Joi Maria Probus, and Yvonne Aguirre. And last but by no means least, to my publicist, Sandy Lawrence and her team which included my son, David Little and Martine Lewis, thank you for all your creativity and support.

I have been married to the same woman for thirty-three years, and I could not have written this book without Melinda's love and support. I have three wonderful adult children, and a great son-in-law, and without their support I would not have finished this book, or anything else.

I must also thank my parents, David and Maurine Little. When my first-grade teacher, Mrs. Letts, told them not to punish me because I told so many stories all the time, and that I would write a book someday, they listened to her.

# TABLE OF CONTENTS

# CHAPTER 1

Ava walked to the oak double front doors and stretched. It took longer and longer to loosen up, and it hurt. It hurt because she was forty, and no matter how good she looked, she knew time was taking its toll on her body. It hurt because Don's idiocy stressed her out. She couldn't figure out what to do about him. She walked onto the expansive front porch, plugged her earphones in, clicked on her playlist, and then slowly jogged over the green lawn and up the empty street lined with similar homes before crossing a lonely intersection and entering the park.

She jogged her usual route—a well-manicured gravel trail that wound through the heavy forest of large oaks and cypress, with a dense tropical underbrush of two-inch-thick wild muscadine grapevines reaching up into the canopy. Ava concentrated on her running and listening to her own breathing even over her music, letting its rhythm regulate her run. She couldn't hear the loud crunch of gravel each step made as she ran, but for the birds and insects, her even footfalls were the only sounds in the park on the early, crisp morning.

Alex Jimenez kicked the stack of dirty clothes and pulled out a long-sleeved plaid shirt. He took a quick armpit sniff and put it on anyway. The fabric stuck to his sweaty body as he tugged it on. He looked around his small room with its scarred brown walls and water-stained ceiling for his steel-toed boots, and when he didn't see them, he got on his knees and knocked around the piles of fast-food bags and dirty clothes while cockroaches scattered until he found the boots. He popped his radio on and turned it up when he heard Diablo playing. He sipped from an old beer he'd opened the night before and checked his new burner for the time: 5:30 a.m. He jumped at seeing it, finished the beer in a gulp, and tossed the empty can in the corner. He couldn't screw this job up. He didn't have any options left. No one would give him a fucking job when they found out he was a felon, and the damn state wouldn't give him welfare. Besides, nobody wanted to hire him when they saw the two teardrops tattooed down the side of his face—no one until she walked up to him at Colinas a couple of weeks ago.

A pretty white woman in her little shiny dress; when she sat on the barstool next to him, he thought he'd take her, and then she spoke. "I'm Melody Jones," she said, and everything changed. She wasn't beautiful— pretty, he'd thought at first—but after he got to know her, he didn't give a shit anymore. She talked, and he locked on whatever she said. He could barely remember what she said really, but at the time he concentrated on it—she just talked so much. That part hurt his head. Alex kept his hands to himself, said "yes, ma'am" for the first fucking time since ever, and acted like he agreed with whatever she said. He couldn't believe someone like her even talked to someone like him, and she knew some things about him—how, he had no idea. He was afraid to ask her questions like that. She mentioned names he knew, but it didn't matter; he just wanted her to keep talking to him. She had sat down, but she wouldn't drink a beer when he asked. She said she heard he was looking for a job, and to impress her he told her he had one.

"Doing what?" She didn't believe him. A fancy woman with an expensive purse he'd steal if it weren't hers. He was surprised that she wasn't afraid of him—and glad, too.

"Your friends say you can be trusted," she said.

Yeah, he doubted anybody told her that. He didn't have any friends, but since she said it, he wanted to believe it. He said of course he could, all his friends knew that. That's what he thinks he said. He's not sure. She told him to meet her later at Moody Park down the block, and he agreed he would. But he didn't want her to leave. As she walked out, all eyes in the ice house watched that butt.

Alex waited an hour at the park for her to show up. He wouldn't have put up with that from any other bitch, but he was excited to see her again, so he waited. Hell, it was an honor just to be around her. She finally pulled up in a black Mercedes, honked, and motioned for him to get in. That shocked him again—letting him in her car. He jumped in, and she took off.

"What's this about?" he asked.

"I need a job done—" she started.

He didn't know where she was driving or what road they were on; all he could see was this blonde with a nice body. She could lose a little though—and that dress rising high on her leg. He still wanted her, couldn't keep his eyes off her body, and she didn't seem to mind him looking. But it was more than that. He wanted to please her, make her happy. If she wanted him to do something, some job, whatever it was, he was going to do it.

Turned out the job was something he'd already done twice—kill. That surprised him—why would somebody like her need anybody killed? But why else would someone like her want to be his friend? And if he did a good job, he might get to be around her more.

After he agreed, they met three more times—not dates, but to talk about his money. She told him her plan, drove him to see the trail, and showed him a picture of the bitch he was going to kill there. When she dropped him at Moody the last time yesterday, she said, "Do it tomorrow, and I'll meet you here a week after it's done." Then he watched her drive off.

Alex grabbed the worn, black .22 hidden under dirty jeans and shoved it in his front pocket. She gave him enough money for a bigger gun, told him to buy a .38 or better, but he spent that money and stole this piece of crap, but it'd be good enough. He tried to run to the Fulton North Central rail, but after one parking lot he got tired and walked the three blocks.

He missed the first train and waited for the next. He'd told Ms. Melody he needed money for a cab, but she told him "no," it could be traced. As he waited he thought about calling one anyway and lying to her, but he was afraid she might be right.

When the next rail finally slid to a stop in front of him, he stepped on and saw he was the only passenger. He settled into a seat, checking the time on his phone repeatedly as the red line eased to a stop to take on passengers and then slipped forward with its fresh payload. The new train smelled new, a cheap, overly air-conditioned model. He wished his apartment smelled that good.

Downtown, he jumped on an express bus headed for Memorial; already six people on this one, working people. The kind he'd expect to see riding down to the rich part of town. Two men wore work uniforms, and four women were dressed to clean someone else's house all day. The bus didn't stop, but took I-10 straight to the Villages, then started making stops once it got to Bunker Hill. Alex had only been to this strange part of town once, and that was when Miss Melody drove him over there to show him the bitch's house and the trail at the park next to it. The whole place was a foreign country that Alex wasn't allowed into. He figured that if he tried to live there, if he could have afforded it, they'd sic their rich people police on him. He didn't trust them, none of them, except Miss Melody. She was different.

The bus kept stopping, and the other passengers got off. When it stopped at the park Miss Melody showed him, Alex jumped out the back door and ran into the trees. He hurried down the winding path to the spot she told him to ambush the bitch from and crawled on top of the black metal picnic table to wait. Alex leaned back on one arm and flicked his burning cigarette butt at the garbage can. Missed. The gravel trail ran right past him, and he was in the perfect place just like Miss Melody said. He lit another cigarette as he looked at the freshly cut grass picked clean of any trash—or any sticks even.

The trees surrounding the clearing looked like jungle to him, and he inhaled the smell of cut grass and heavy tree pollen through his cigarette smoke. This was way better than the stacked old garbage smell in the beaten-down park up the street from Colinas. The trash cans were empty here, and they had black plastic bags on them. Alex never saw that before, park cans with trash bags; these people were treated right.

He flicked his butt at the trash can again as he watched a wuss in blue sweats slowly run into the clearing, look at Alex and the butt as it hit the grass, and speed up as he passed by. Alex laughed at it, the thought of a man giving up sleep to run in a park. "Dumbass," he thought. He was glad the pussy hurried, and he hoped the guy got far enough away before he popped the bitch.

He had to stay ready. Once he shot her, he'd get some breakfast tacos. There's a truck a couple of blocks from his room that he bought tacos from late at night. They were good, too, especially the green salsa they made, and he wondered if they were open this early. Of course they were. He hoped that guy was far enough away. He checked the time on his phone again. He'd waited too long for the bitch, and he worried he'd missed her. He might go to Colinas after lunch for a beer to celebrate. He'd have some money coming in so they'd probably give him credit; they'd have to since he'd already spent everything she'd advanced him. If he did this woman well enough, he might get some of Miss Melody, too, and stop having to call her that Miss shit.

A blond woman with headphones ran past him. Who was that? He panicked. Was that her? Blond chick, like in the picture—it had to be. He jumped off the table, jerked his gun out of his pants, and ran after her.

"That was scary," she thought. She usually ran thinking only of breathing, the next mile, and the song in her ear. She ran on this trail four days a week, and she didn't even think about it or what was around her in the park—she just ran. It was the only time she could escape her problem, and she loved running. She came around a turn, and this big guy in old clothes was sitting on top of a picnic table smoking a cigarette waiting—for what?

When she first saw him, she lost her breath, but she just kept running at the same pace. As she passed right by him, she peeked over to make sure he didn't jump at her, and though he didn't even look at her—he ignored her like he didn't even see her—she saw two teardrops tattooed on the side of his face. Ava didn't know what that meant, but it made her lose her breath again, and she sped up to get away so suddenly that she wrenched one of her earphones out. Once out of the clearing and around a couple of turns, she began to calm down and relax, even if she was still jogging.

"What's a guy like that doing in this park?" she wondered. She saw neighbors running in the park in the mornings, occasionally an old couple rising early for a slow walk while it was still cool, but no one outside her neighborhood came to her park, not when she'd ever been here.

She heard a pop and immediately saw a tiny piece of bark snap off a tree as she ran by it. "What was that? That's strange," she thought.

"Damn."

She heard a man's voice shout behind her, and when she turned her head to look back at who yelled, she saw the scary man from the picnic table pointing a gun at her. She screamed as loud as she could, and she took off running as fast as she could possibly run, faster than she ever ran, screaming, "Help, help," as she ran. As she cut a corner, her earphones caught on a branch and along with her phone were ripped from her body, but she didn't dare look back for them.

Another shot—she heard it this time, knew what it was. He was shooting at her while he chased her. As she ran, two sets of feet crashed the gravel. She listened like a hunted rabbit to identify where her hunter was, if he was trying to cut her off, and if anyone else called out after they heard her screams.

"Please, please, hear me," she silently prayed. She twisted around a tree and then another turn, and then stopped screaming so her predator couldn't hear where she was, but she breathed so hard and loud that she knew he would hear anyway. Then she realized he might already be cutting through the bushes to grab her. She ran this trail all the time, so she remembered where she was and cut through the brush, smashing by bushes and vines and around trees.

She stopped again, didn't hear any more shots or any other sound from him; she didn't know where he was anymore, but she was too scared now to listen or even think. In total panic, she crashed through the jungle, making as straight a line as possible away from where she thought he was and any trap around a turn. Thorns and branches tore across her arms, legs, and face, ripping her flesh, but she couldn't feel it—she just ran. Something jerked her shirt, and she tore it away as she fled. Her ankle hit a hard log; she stumbled but she refused to fall, and without a cry of sound at the pain, she caught herself and ran on. The trail wrapped back around in front of her, and as she stepped onto it, she saw a man jogging away.

"Help," she risked screaming.

When he turned, he froze at the look of her, and then he ran up to her and said, "What's happened? You're bleeding all over."

"Help me." She grabbed him so he couldn't leave. "Please, there's a man chasing me with a gun. He's trying to kill me. Please help me; I'm so scared. I'm so scared."

The bitch was gone, Alex thought as he sat on his knees trying to get a breath, any breath. Sweat crawled down his face. She'd snuck past him before he realized it was her. He'd chased her down despite being in these damn boots he'd been so stupid as to wear; they were like a pound of mud on each foot. He'd almost caught her before she knew he was behind her. His chest hurt like a fucking heart attack. Then his shitty gun went off and shot a fucking tree. He should've used some of the damn money for a better gun. When the bitch saw his ass, she ran off like a cartoon-screaming crazy. It woulda been funny if she hadn't got away.

He tried to stand up, but he still couldn't breathe enough and he was too weak. He felt like his legs were buried in the ground. He spit and force himself to stand. His side hurt like she'd stabbed him with a knife in the ribs twice, grinding the bone. He loved doing that. He knew what it felt like, too, and she might as well have done it by getting away. That bitch ruined everything.

He lit a cigarette as he walked back the way he came, wiping the sweat running down his face and neck with his hands until he took off his shirt to use as a rag.

"Damn." What was he going to tell Miss Melody? He walked back to the bus stop and looked around at the big houses with their doors and windows. There were people in all of them, people he hated, and somebody was probably staring at him right now wondering what that scum was doing in their park, so he turned around and hid in the woods.

# CHAPTER 2

The elevator door opened, and Larry checked the crowded lobby to search whether Lar was there. Thank God, he wasn't. Relieved he was alone, Larry worked his way through the busy men and women rushing around him checking out or moving luggage. He didn't hear Lar's voice in the roar of people made up of many familiar faces.

"Good morning, Mr. Lamb," said a young porter and the concierge.

"Good morning." Larry enjoyed their greeting every morning. It wasn't like living at home—if he was allowed to anymore—and having Diane and his little girl and boy to kiss him good morning, but it was nice. He lived in this hotel instead of moving into a high-rise in his deluded hope that Diane would wake up one morning and miraculously forgive him, accept that he was well, and tell him to come home. That's what he waited for—to watch his children play on their swing set in his backyard again.

That's the way it had always been during their marriage before Diane's boob job and his screw up. "Now it's your turn; lose a hundred pounds," she'd said.

"Your car will be around in just a moment, Mr. Lamb. Would you like a coffee or espresso while you wait?" said the head valet.

"Thanks." Larry gave him a five as he waited.

When he didn't lose the weight, Diane gave him the number for Nguyen Weight Clinic—a little office in an old strip center with a nasty parking lot. "Now, we'll call these prescriptions in to your pharmacies, but you'll have to give us the names of two pharmacies. We'll call half into each," the nurse said. He knew why.

The pills worked, too, but not the way he'd expected. He mixed the contents of the leather case of pill bottles he carried around with the vodka he just didn't seem to get off, and he stopped sleeping and eating, except the 3:00 a.m. four cheeseburgers. One 3:00 a.m., Larry saw Lar for the first time watching from a car in the street in front of Larry's home. Lar was nothing but a dark shadow then, but Larry knew Lar was watching. When Larry drove down his driveway to confront the shadow, he was gone.

Larry's silver Lexus screeched to a stop, and the young kid popped out and held the door open. Larry headed to the office. After first seeing Lar as a shadow watching the house from the street in the middle of the night, Larry began hearing a sound behind a wall in his den.

"There's nothing there, Larry. Stop drinking while you're taking all those pills," Diane said.

"I'm not." He lied. She knew.

"Please come back upstairs and sleep with me."

"No. I'll sit here in my chair. I can't sleep, and I'll keep you awake."

During that time, David, his law partner, asked Larry to substitute for him on a onetime-only court appearance for a new client. The joke they both laughed at was that Larry didn't go to court anymore, didn't know how to practice law anymore, and he didn't do anything but sit in his office and stare at his investments' minutiae changes on a computer screen. But David needed his help, it was a simple misdemeanor anyway, and all he had to do was get a reset of a hearing, so even Larry might be able to do it. He couldn't.

It was an indecent exposure charge in a little, dusty, rural county, Waller, west of Houston, with a little, brown courthouse. The sheriff's deputies and judge couldn't have been more stereotypical if they were invented by a Manhattan writer. When Larry arrived in the courtroom, the clerk sent him to the jail, a dirty one-story box, to talk to his client. Brian Bain was a panicked twenty-five-year-old street kid from Houston that got caught on a ten-minute date with what he thought was just a cowboy, but turned out to be an undercover cop—at least that's what the deputy called himself afterward.

When Larry sat down in the cell to explain to Brian he'd be stuck in jail at least two more weeks because his real lawyer was making more money at another courthouse in another county this morning—without actually saying those words—Brian burst into tears.

"Thank you. Thank you so much for helping me." And then he vomited out how he was going to be murdered and Larry had to get him out and rescue him.

"Wait. What are you talking about? I'm just going to reset your case." Larry didn't have the courage or knowledge to help.

"No. No. You can't. You've got to get me out before they find out I'm here."

"Look. No one gives a shit about you. No one's going to kill you." Larry was going to kill David for dumping this on him.

"Yes, they do. No, I know. You heard about John Snow?"

"No." He had, but he didn't want to go down this line.

"Well, when he finds out I'm in this rattrap, I'm totally fucked. You've got to get me out of here so I can hide."

Trapped, Larry returned to the courtroom and stumbled about asking other attorneys who were waiting on their own cases to be heard and even the court's clerk until he figured out how to ask the judge for a lower bail, and shockingly, the judge granted his request.

Brian's old, heartbroken mother hugged him outside the courtroom before she even introduced herself. "Oh, Mr. Larry, thank you so much. You saved my son. You saved his life." She smelled like faded mothballs.

"Ma'am, you're welcome." He tried to disentangle himself. "Just have him call David when he gets out."

"Oh no, Mr. Larry, he owes you everything. He's staying with you." She continued to hang on him, and he was now so overwhelmed by her gratitude for his stupid legal stumbling that it humbled him.

"It's OK, Mrs. Bain; David's my partner, and I was just here for this one time."

"No, sir, he has to stay with you. My boy's life depends on it."

"Then he's in trouble," Larry thought, "because I don't know shit."

Larry took a breath as he drove. Peace now. That's what he had. He'd lost the weight and most of the cigarettes. Brian was dead. Only one problem might prevent Diane from calling him, and no one knew about Lar anymore. Everyone believed Larry was well, and he was, really. He was in control and almost home.

As he stepped into his office, Suzy hung up the phone behind the receptionist desk and said, "You have a ten thirty. I was afraid you wouldn't make it."

"That's your fault," he said as he walked by. "You know better than to schedule me so early."

"David's looking for you," she said as he walked down the long hall to his office at the end.

Linda, David's secretary, said as he walked by her cubicle, "David'll take it if you don't want it."

"Of course I don't want it." It was the game they played. He was so famous from Brian's case that every petty criminal now thought he was some kind of superlawyer and they wanted to hire him, but he just handed them off to David, like now. He owed David that for saving his life so many times over the last year.

"I'll take the ten thirty," David said from his office as Larry passed.

"I know."

Larry closed his office door behind him, sat at his desk, turned on his computers, looked across his desk, and his throat constricted into a tight knot. Lar was sitting there and waiting.

"You weren't at the hotel," Larry said once his throat relaxed enough for air to barely go through it.

"*Nothing there. Sitting out on the balcony drinking coffee and reminiscing. What's that shit?*" Lar said.

"It was nice. I was alone."

*"I'm here now."*

"I know, but it doesn't matter anymore because I know you're not real."

*"I'm real enough."*

"But I know I just see you. Since you're not real, I don't have to worry about you killing me anymore."

*"Just because I'm not real, what makes you think I'm not going to kill you?"*

# CHAPTER 3

"**Q**aam per wapis jayo. Miyhe poor raat yahan nahi rehna hai," yelled the boss.

"Main qaam per hoon. Miyhe akele ko ye sab kerna hay, is lieye waqt lag raha hai. It's not like you ever wait until I'm finished," Ahmed Bawany said. Every night, after the Bashmillah closed, Ahmed scrubbed the café clean, and his fat, young boss left to meet his friends at the clubs in the Gandhi District. The kid didn't respect Ahmed because he was an old man that cleaned the child's family's café, and the kid was eager to let Ahmed know it.

"Theek Hai. Barabar raaf kar ley na. My friends are waiting for me. Make sure it's clean," the boss said as he locked Ahmed in the café and left.

"Make sure it's clean? Every morning, it's the cleanest restaurant in Houston," Ahmed thought, but that boy wasn't awake until after the lunch crowd left, so he never knew. By the time that kid got to work, Ahmed already had slept a little and was at his day job. That child would've treated him differently if they were back home; there, Ahmed was an engineer and fought in Kashmir. Here, he worked where he could for cash. Whether building mountain fortifications in the Himalayas or cleaning this floor, Ahmed worked properly and without complaint. He had to save his sons. Who'd think they'd be in more danger in America than in their country torn by civil war and terrorism? Ahmed brought them here to get a good education and make real money, but they joined a gang instead, and within a month were arrested for transporting and selling pounds of some drug. Ahmed didn't really understand which one because he refused to understand any of it. All he knew was the shame, the murdering, the painful shame and heartache that his sons would spend the rest of their lives in prison. His wife had already given up on life and was waiting for death, but he couldn't.

The woman offered him an alternative—hope and hell. He'd go to hell for what he agreed to do for her. Donna Smith—she couldn't think of a better lie than that name? Smith's clumsy deceit gave Ahmed reason to doubt she could rescue his sons. He didn't even know what her hair color was under that cheap wig, but he knew it didn't have blond roots, though he believed she had the contacts, the influence, to somehow get his sons out. Ahmed didn't understand the American system and he was too ashamed to ask his countrymen, but a woman like her had the power to get anyone to do what she wanted—Ahmed knew that much. He'd learned how to read people.

But in return, he must do the unthinkable. The next day, he drove to the place Smith had showed him, put on the lime-green work jacket she gave him, and with the 9mm in his pocket unloaded the wheelbarrow and shovel from his pickup. He rolled into the woods to the trail she showed him and began acting like he was filling holes with dirt. He accidently stepped in horse manure; it littered the trail, but the disgusting filth made him appear authentic. "Qismat aaj meri hai," he said out loud. He was too ashamed to think what God thought.

He shivered as he pulled the unfortunate lady's picture from his pocket to remind himself, though Miss Smith repeatedly showed him a video of her riding her big red horse, so he knew exactly what she looked like. The puzzle to Ahmed was he knew more about the lady on the horse than Miss Smith, but still he was ready. When he fought in Kashmir, he did much worse, but they were soldiers, not a woman. He had no alternative; he must do whatever it took to save his sons regardless of her horrific demand.

"Saddle my baby," Ava ordered as the waiter served dessert and coffee. Too slow and gentle for the track, Joe was a tall, red thoroughbred gelding and made the prettiest riding horse at the club. He was more Ava's pet than her horse, and he loved her. After she finished lunch with her friends, who left to take care of their families, she rode Joe. The staff laughed because she pampered him more than rode him, and he wiggled up to her like a Yorkie when she approached him.

"That horse is fat. You need to let us exercise him," the staff complained. Good, conscientious people, but they wouldn't touch her Joe. He was all she had left, and she wouldn't let anyone work him when she wasn't there. Ava walked him to the edge of the trail where they were alone, fed him his expected treat, and then slowly rode into the woods.

She was too frightened to run in the park anymore even though the police immediately caught the horrible thief who attacked her. Here, there were people in the club and stable employees around the trails, and she sat high on Joe. No one knew where she was but Bruce and her friends, and she had to get on with her life. She was safe.

Ava and Joe lingered down the narrow, sandy trails through the pines. The mix from the trail, tree pollen, and Joe was her favorite smell, more than any of her perfumes, and neither wanted to hurry their time together. Occasionally, they'd pass a couple of riders, but they had most of the trails to themselves. She didn't think; she just petted Joe and forgot her problems.

They turned into an opening and approached a worker in a green stable jacket filling holes. Joe slowed and edged sideways away from the man, and Ava laid her hand on his neck and whispered to him that he was OK. As she eased Joe past him, Ava saw in the corner of her eye the man drop the shovel and pull a gun out of his jacket. The shovel hit the ground with a loud ping at the same time Ava jerked the reins in panic, and Joe swung around to face the man, raised up on his back legs, and jumped at him. The gun fired, and the hollow point bullet burst through Joe's chest. Blood spewed out as Joe collapsed to his side, pulling up just long enough for Ava to pull her leg out of the stirrup and avoid being crushed beneath him.

The man dodged the falling horse as he was sprayed with its blood. Joe screamed his last breath, and the man ran away and back into the woods. Ava saw him disappear, heard yells from people coming, and sobbing, fell onto the neck of her savior as he died.

# CHAPTER 4

It was Don Stonek's habit to pace when he was nervous or scared. He took his usual path along the wall of windows that was the focal point of the expansive penthouse. The view of Houston calmed him down, centered him. He paused before the first window and ran his fingers through a mass of black hair. He took in his physique—still tall and muscular, belying his age of fifty-three. His body refused to cave to the demands of being the CEO of the world's third largest oil-field servicing company, Windam Pipe & Servicing.

He enjoyed his women outside Houston until a woman walked into a party with all the gravity and power Jesus Christ would have. After he met Marilyn, there were no other women anywhere, except Ava. That was the problem. Don took Marilyn to restaurants and his club, and that infuriated his wife. Her tirade that it stop enraged Marilyn, who then, to Don's disbelief, was arrested for hiring men to shoot at his wife. The press repeated every rumor about the love triangle of the powerful man, his high society wife, and the girlfriend charged with attempted capital murder.

"You need to stay out of it," said John Ulm, a silver-haired attorney, as he sat listening to Stonek panic. Ulm's firm handled all of Stonek's personal and Windam's business issues, and it made Ulm very wealthy. He was not going to lose his cash cow because his client didn't think.

"I've got to get her a lawyer," Stonek said.

"It'll make you a bigger target." Ulm sipped his coffee.

"I didn't know Marilyn would do it."

"I didn't say you did."

"And if I don't get her someone, and someone good, she'll think I abandoned her." Stonek choked as he laughed, "And then all hell could break loose."

"Is there any way she could implicate you in this harebrained scheme?"

"No, you've known me for fifteen years, John; there's no way I'd ever put up with that."

"You never heard her talk about it in anyway?"

"We've talked about this before, John. I've told you, Marilyn was angry with Ava's fit, but there was no discussion about the rest of it."

"It wouldn't be wise to allow the district attorney to discover you hired her attorney. The press is already wild."

Don paced his route again and said, "Move on. Who do we hire?"

Having covered himself by warning Stonek about the dangers, Ulm said, "There are a couple in town, big enough and good enough, to handle something like this."

Stonek shook his head. "No, I don't want that. I just want someone that she'll think can save her so she won't start making shit up."

Ulm took a drink and stared at Don.

"Do you know someone like that?"

Neither one of them spoke for a couple of minutes, and then Ulm said, "I may know someone."

"Who?"

"Remember about six months ago when the DA came up with that crazy theory about John Snow?"

"Oh yeah, that guy was the worst fucking businessman."

"And that young man was the DA's witness?"

"Until he wasn't."

"The boy's attorney got a lot of press. The reporters treated him on-air like a genius."

"What's his name?"

"I don't know. Lamb something, I think. He's incompetent, but since he's so famous in Houston right now, she might believe you took care of her."

Don slowly lowered himself into the chair behind his desk. "Check up on this guy, but you've got to move fast before she does something stupid."

"I'll sit down with him, see if he fits our need."

The buzzing speaker of the office phone jarred Larry from his trance. He'd been closed off in his office since he got to work that day, researching online how to keep track of Diane. He slapped a button on the phone. "Yeah."

"John Ulm for you."

"Who?"

"John Ulm."

That couldn't be right. Larry knew that name. He was one of the most powerful attorneys in Houston. There was no way he would have a reason to call Larry. He picked up the phone and said, "Larry Lamb."

"Good afternoon, Mr. Lamb. I'm John Ulm. I hope I'm not interrupting you from something important."

"No, no, just working on some cases."

"We've never met, but I hoped you could drop by my office after work and have a drink. I think I may have a case for you."

Larry doubted it. John Ulm represented huge corporations and dealt with complicated problems. He had packs of attorneys to do his work. Larry didn't even want to bother with that type of work—or any work really. He also planned on driving to his house, seeing Diane, watching Danny's basketball game, and being with his family.

"I have a lot of work to do. I was going to be here pretty late," Larry said.

"Oh, come on over. You'll be glad you did. It's a serious case with a serious retainer." Then, to sweeten the invitation, he said, "I know that you make plenty, but this involves a pretty big case, it's getting a ton of press, and you'd be on the news every night."

"Who is it?"

"Just come on over. About seven thirty?"

Larry had to go. You don't tell John Ulm no, and he wanted to see what his offices looked like. When he hung up, he walked to the door of David's office.

David looked up from his work and said, "I heard John Ulm called you."

"Yeah."

"Damn. What'd he lower himself to call you about?"

"He wanted me to come have a drink with him at his office tonight. He said he has a case for me."

"You?"

"Yeah." Larry knew John Ulm didn't have a case for or care about Larry. It could've been a joke or something else, so he had David's assistant confirm.

"He said it's been in the press every day. What's been on the local news? I've been too busy to watch."

"Busy doing what?"

"Busy."

"Bullshi…" David drew it out. "I don't know anything on the news you could handle: murders and burglaries. Some woman was arrested for hiring men to kill some socialite; that's what's been all over the local television."

"That wouldn't be it."

"He might represent the socialite's family."

"So, why would he want me on something like that?"

"Why would he want you at all?"

Ulm's downtown law offices occupied the thirty-eighth through the fortieth floors of its building, with a reception area of crystal window doors, marble tile, and Oriental rugs. Original modern art hung in the waiting room and down the visible hall.

A cute blonde—everyone here apparently worked later than Larry's office—walked him back to Ulm. Associates' offices he passed still had attorneys and paralegals as busy as if it were midafternoon. She knocked on the door at the end of the second hall, opened it, and stepped aside for Larry to enter.

"Mr. Ulm, Mr. Lamb."

Larry walked in to a man coming around his desk. A young woman and man, both in attorneys' suits, stood up smiling, but silent. The office was expensively furnished in old lawyer style—leather and dark mahogany. It was very neat—no stacks of books or files. It appeared Larry was right—Ulm didn't do any of his own work.

"Nice to finally meet you, Mr. Lamb." He looked just like the Internet pictures Larry checked—big, tall, white-haired guy with a big nose like old men get, and a big belly covered up with a five-thousand-dollar suit. They shook hands, Ulm's swallowing Larry's. "I've looked so forward to meeting you."

Larry doubted that. "It's nice to meet you, too," he said as the door shut behind him. Larry and Ulm sat down in a separate lounge area of the office. Larry sank into a huge, buttery-soft leather couch like a toddler. Ulm sat on the edge of the chair next to him, and his two minions sat back down where they were, but extremely attentive to what was said. A redhead came in, asked what Larry drank, and left.

Ulm asked him about his family, how his son's basketball was going, and how his law practice was. The redhead returned with their drinks and left again.

"Larry"—Ulm suggested they use their first names since he hoped they'd become friends—"I'm glad you could break away to come up here tonight because I have a very important case and I need your help."

*"You don't believe that crap, do you?"* asked Lar, who sat next to Larry, lounging comfortably and not looking ridiculous on the couch. Larry grimaced and thought to Lar, "What are you doing here now?"

"Are you OK?" asked Ulm.

"I'm fine."

*"You're whacked,"* Lar said.

Larry took a drink from the crystal whiskey glass, Crown, not the normal stuff—black, nice glass—and he concentrated on the irrelevancies to relax and make Lar leave.

"Larry, I'm sure you've seen the news about the lady, a Miss Ramirez, who was arrested a few days ago for attempted capital murder?" Ulm slouched back in his chair, pretending not to care so much about what he was talking about.

"No, I haven't—working you know; my partner mentioned it."

Lar was gone.

"Well, this woman was arrested and charged with hiring two men to kill Ava Stonek. Have you ever met Mrs. Stonek?" Ulm was really pretending not to care about this.

"No, but I've heard of her; everyone has." Larry slid up to the edge of the couch so his feet could touch the floor, and he concentrated on what Ulm said to make Lar stay away.

"That's who Miss Ramirez is accused of trying to have killed. It's a big case. Whoever represents her will be famous in this town, and after, frankly, your brilliant representation of Bain, I can't think of anyone more capable of representing her."

This isn't what Larry thought he was here to talk about. The Stoneks were the ones with all the money, not a nobody sitting in county jail.

*"Bain's dead. You killed him."* Lar was back.

"Get out," thought Larry, and then he said, "Why are you hiring her attorney? So, you represent her?" as he sipped his drink, looked straight at Ulm, and made sure he couldn't see any of the couch in his peripheral vision.

"Can I freshen that for you?" Ulm said as he stood up and glanced at Larry's empty glass.

"I'm fine."

"No. If you take this case, my firm's involvement must remain confidential. I represent a third party that believes in Miss Ramirez's innocence and wants to make sure she gets the best legal counsel possible."

"Bullshit, it's something else, and he knows we know it's something else, so what is it?" Larry thought as he waited.

"If you'll agree to take the case and to my confidentiality, I'll put one hundred fifty thousand in your trust fund as a retainer, and pay your fee at six hundred dollars an hour, plus expenses, on a monthly basis."

"Frankly, Mr. Ulm—"

"John."

"I'm not really sure I'm the right guy." He didn't know anything about criminal law, much less attempted capital murder, or the procedures in court he'd have to follow if he took the case. The money was worth the trouble though. Ulm was talking more than half a million before it was over, and Larry could use it; he'd spent a third of his money already.

*"They're setting you up, dumbass,"* Lar said.

"They who?" thought Larry.

"Of course, my associates"—Ulm looked at his two toadies—"can help you in any way you need: prepare documents, procedures, words to use, everything."

The brunette crossed her legs.

That solves a problem, and David could help.

*"That's not what the setup is, but do it, do it,"* Lar said.

He probably wouldn't have to litigate it. These things never go to trial, not often.

*"Do it."*

Ulm said, "Time is really crucial, Larry. She needs someone now. She's already been in jail awhile; no telling what they've tricked her into saying."

*"Do it."*

"Is your friend worried about that?" Larry asked.

"No, but we both know how the police can be."

"That's true."

*"He knows about your ass in jail,"* Lar said.

Before Larry learned what Lar actually was, Larry was twice arrested because of him. Larry thought Lar and Diane were trying to kill him and that Lar was following him waiting for the chance. Larry crashed his car both times fleeing Lar, the first time managing to get arrested for DWI as well as beat up by a cop. The second arrest was worse.

"Lar is right," thought Larry.

*"Gettin' upset now, aren't you? You've quit thinking. Good."*

"Fuck off," Larry thought. Why shouldn't he talk to her? He could talk to her. That wouldn't hurt. "I'll have to speak to my partner," he said.

Ulm smiled. "Of course you do—we all do—but you need to get down there right away, tonight, so she knows she's not alone."

*"The fat man's excited now. Look at him; he knows he's closed on you."*

"I'll go down first thing in the morning. Do you know when her next hearing is?" said Larry, and the brunette acted like she wanted to answer.

"I'll pay you now, but you'll have to go down there tonight. She needs your help. Miss Wiley and Mr. Miller will drive you. You don't want to park around the jail this time of night."

"Pressure. That's part of taking the money if I say yes," Larry thought. He said, "I only answer to her if I do it. You might write checks, but you're out besides that. It'll just be her and her best interest." He thought, "Maybe that will get him to say no."

"Of course."

"And if I take it, I have to tell her how I'm getting paid."

"Of course."

*"Yeah, dumbass, that's the signal."*

Larry knew he should have insisted on knowing who was paying, but it didn't matter. After he talked to her, he'd reject it. It was just that it was so much money. And as long as he took care of her, it didn't matter anyway. No one would ever know.

Ulm stood up like his job was done, buzzed an assistant, and walked out. When the assistant came in, it was a different young woman in a tighter skirt. She brought Larry a cup of coffee the way he liked it—how she knew, he had no idea—followed by Ulm carrying a check.

"My associates will let me know how your meeting goes with Miss Ramirez."

"What's her first name?"

"Marilyn."

# CHAPTER 5

It was hot and sticky and dark, and Larry was stuck working. The two infants working for Ulm drove him to the jail in the back of Mr. Miller's Audi sedan. From the front seat Ms. Wiley reached over and handed him a thick file, a detailed outline of the facts known and the possible laws and procedures that might be available to Miss Ramirez. "It also has, if you'll turn to the third section," Ms. Wiley instructed, "suggestions on what you'll want to do in the next two days."

It was as if they knew Larry would be sitting in this backseat at this moment with them headed to the jail. The car crossed the bridge from downtown and turned onto a street in a canyon lined with tall, Soviet-bloc buildings—all jails. They stopped at the sixth. "His spin number is here." Ms. Wiley reached over the seat again and pointed with her manicured nail on the top right corner of the outside of the file. "You'll need to show them your driver's license and bar card."

"I know," he said as he got out.

"We'll be here when you come out."

"You better be." This was no place to wait for a cab at 11:00 p.m., and they'd want their report as to why he'd refused to take the case. The air had an oppressive, dark sense even with the weird fluorescent lights, like an old '60s Orson Welles Kafka movie.

Larry pulled open the gigantic metal door, walked through layers of security to the inner lobby edifice, and pushed the button on a console to speak to a deputy behind thick bulletproof glass. He pushed it three times before the answer came. "We're closed." He argued with two deputies and a supervisor before they agreed to allow him to speak to his client and clicked open two more security doors. These guys matched the building, as though they were all from some southern part of the old Soviet Union. It wasn't like they were doing anything but drinking coffee. It was funny how diverse Houston was—not stereotypical—and then Larry had to argue with these guys. He stepped into the box; it's called an attorney-client conference room, but it's a box. A cement box. The last time he'd been in a room like this, he'd been on the other side of the table and freaking out.

"I'm not going to keep bailing you out like this, Larry," David said then.

"I know. I know."

"What happened this time? Why'd you take the kids? You could've killed them."

"I know now." That's because Lar spoke to him that night for the first time. He was no longer just a shadow following Larry, haunting him, or driving a car trying to run him down, but Larry never admitted that to David. "I realize now I was just imagining it. I need help."

The echo of steel doors slamming in distant parts of the floor brought Larry back to the present and told him she was moving his way. A fat man's face flashed in the tiny window in the door, and then it clicked open. A short, heavy woman of about forty stepped in. She had greasy, dark hair. She probably was pretty once. This wouldn't take even as long as he'd thought.

"Hi," she said. She was so unafraid. Late at night the guards roust her to this little metal and concrete box, and she says "Hi."

"I'm Marilyn Ramirez. Are you my lawyer?"

Yes, he might be. He needed to answer her. "Say something," he thought to himself.

"I'm Larry Lamb. I'm an attorney."

She scraped a metal chair across the concrete toward the table. It echoed off the bare walls, and she smiled. She sat and brushed her oily hair back with her hand, and then she blushed. "Did the court appoint you?" So innocent. Larry smiled, as if he was qualified enough to ever be appointed in a case this big by the court. The jail kept the air-conditioning high in this room—you could hear it roar, the clammy coldness meant to freeze out long attorney-client meetings—and the room smelled like bleach guards gave trustees to clean the human filth a thousand locked-up humans made.

"No. No, I was asked by someone else, obviously a friend of yours, to come talk to you and make sure you're OK." He paused for just a beat to take a breath and measure his words before he continued, "And that you get an attorney, that your rights are protected." He didn't intend to tell her about Ulm—unless he took the case.

She sat looking into him and listening like what he said was the most important thing she could hear, and he felt truly important to her—vital. "Who?" she said, and his intentions crumbled just that easily.

"An attorney in town. He's representing someone unknown…"

"Who is it?"

"John Ulm." She wanted to know, and he wanted to make her happy. As she watched him, he noticed how well the oversize orange jail overalls fit her.

"Will you help me, Mr. Lamb?" She didn't ask more questions about Ulm, and she did need help. Someone to protect her from the police, to keep her safe, and to keep her mouth shut so she wouldn't incriminate herself. Larry knew he could do it. He could defend her until he found someone who knew the law, really knew it.

Marilyn sat as confidently as if she sat on a throne, and he admired her for it, but he had to tell her the truth. He didn't want to let her down, and with this thought, Larry felt Lar scratching through the wall Larry built; he leaned against it, braced it, to protect his consciousness, his wall. Scraping like a roofing nail against a blackboard, Lar tried to break out.

"Are you OK, Larry?" She used his first name, and it sounded good.

"Of course I am. I was just thinking what we should do first. I…"

"You twitched." No he didn't.

"I just have to tell you…" Larry leaned forward so she understood how seriously he spoke and to move away from Lar. "I haven't had much experience in criminal court. You might be better off getting a more experienced attorney."

"Look at you, Larry; you're the one."

Now he flushed. "I'll certainly be there for you. We'll need to get someone else for the trial though."

She stretched her hand across the table and laid it softly on his. "I know you'll keep me safe, Larry."

Lar, walled out, relaxed and faded.

"I'll do everything I can. Have you said anything?"

"To the police?"

"Yes."

"No."

"To anyone?" Her answer worried him.

"No. I was waiting on you."

Wow, did that make him happy, and then his cynicism mocked him. "Good. Don't. I'll get into the DA's file tomorrow and see what they have. You say nothing."

"I won't, but aren't you going to ask me what happened?"

Larry remembered he had a file with him, opened it (the mere act cleared his head), and then said, "Miss Ramirez, what's this about?"

"Call me Marilyn."

"OK." He turned to Ms. Wiley's third section. She'd left lines for him to take notes of his interview. He pulled a pen from the binder of the file, clicked it, and said, "Well?"

"You're my attorney. You can't tell anybody anything?" She said it like she didn't know it.

"Of course not."

She leaned to him, her shoulders back. It revealed nothing, but…"They charged me with hiring some guy to hurt some woman."

He knew it; it was more. "It's two guys."

"Yeah, that's what they say, but I don't know what they're talking about, Larry. I didn't ask them to do anything."

"So you know the two guys the police arrested?"

"Their names sounded familiar when that dork mumbled them at me, but I don't remember their names."

"What dork?"

"The cop that kept asking me questions."

"But you know them?"

"I met them—you can't tell."

"I'm not, I told you, but I've got to know everything so there's no surprises."

"I've met them, but I never told anyone to do anything." When she peered at him with that bright face and those invigorating eyes and told him she didn't tell anyone to attack that woman, that was good enough for him. "They might have heard me gripe about her." She grew angry as she spoke, "And got the wrong idea."

"What, you know the woman they tried to kill?"

"I never met her." She lingered through the sentence. It wasn't going to be completely simple to protect Marilyn, but he didn't hesitate in his new conviction to shield her.

Larry checked the file for the name. "But you know Ava Stonek?"

"No. I don't know her." She put too much emphasis on "know," and she was rattled.

Lar banged against the wall, but Larry kept him out. Lar didn't expect Larry would be able to keep him out. Usually, Larry's shaking was Lar's escape key, but Marilyn gave Larry strength, though he knew he had to leave quickly. "We'll talk more about this tomorrow, after I check that file. You just make sure you don't say anything, and if they come get you, tell them I'm your attorney and don't say anything until I'm with you."

"OK, Larry." She smiled as her confidence returned. "You better get some rest tonight, too. Are you sure you're all right?"

"I'm fine. See you tomorrow."

# CHAPTER 6

66 **W**hat *happened? I had shit to say, and I couldn't get in. Good. Represent her. I want you to represent her. She'll eat you up. You don't know shit. You can't handle that woman."* Lar screamed poison all night in Larry's semisleep.

Larry never meant to take her case, and he could feel the honey coating she'd dumped on him drip away by morning. By the time he arrived at his office to tell David what he'd done, he felt more like a tornado survivor—wreckage everywhere around him.

"You can't handle that," David said when Larry told him.

"I know."

"Then what the hell are you doing? You're going to be on every TV in town, you know that?"

When Larry first saw Marilyn, he silently mocked that someone so plain could be accused of tricking, or seducing, two different men to murder, if you could call it that. The two attacks read more like jokes even in Ms. Wiley's dry, sterile brief. Jimenez and Bawany admitted everything about their bumbling attempts, but neither adequately described the woman that told them what to do as looking anything like Marilyn. One wore a wig, but besides that, they might not even be the same woman.

"You're going to fix this, right?" David sat at his desk with his hands on his belly looking at Larry as seriously as he could. He wasn't worried about himself or their irrelevant little firm; he was worried about Larry. That's how he was. He'd rescued Larry when he'd gotten hooked on diet pills and went crazy, and he didn't want to get another call in the middle of the night.

"Of course I am." Larry understood his own stupidity. "I don't know what I'm doing in this anymore than I did with Bain."

"That didn't work out too well."

"David, if I just stay on this, they'll pay a hundred and fifty thousand retainer, and we could make a lot more, and what we can't do, Ulm's office will." Larry finished explaining Ulm's offer.

"And what the hell's that? Someone's setting you up for a butt fuckin'. What do they want? You're crazy agreeing to it." David stood up and leaned over Larry. "The press is going to be all over you. I can't believe you want to jump back into that soup again. You 'bout drowned last time."

"You're right, you're right. I never meant to say yes."

"You couldn't say no to that big-time lawyer." David began to calm down since he'd won the argument, and he sat down.

Larry leaned back in his chair, "No, that wasn't it. I don't give a shit about him. I was going to say no until I met her. My mind kind of just went blank while I was with her."

"What do you mean blank?"

"I don't know. I've never met anyone like her. Before she walked into the cell, I meant to just talk a minute and leave, but…I don't know…something…" Whatever she'd blasted him with, it was gone.

"What's she, a witch? Is she magic?" David said.

"And I'm her slave?" Larry snapped back.

David laughed and yelled, "That's what you're saying."

"Don't deposit the check. I'll just tell her and Ulm the truth: I'm not qualified to handle it, no matter what they say on TV."

"Good. Do it today."

Larry thought that was right, but he had to at least go downtown to see the file, and after that he'd tell Marilyn.

Later that morning Larry drove to the courthouses, a campus of seven new, tall buildings with stone facades to make them appear as old as the original Depression-era building, now mostly used for background for news reports.

Larry walked through the long, synthetically air-conditioned tunnel that connected the garages to all the courthouses to help avoid Houston's heat. As he rode the elevator, his breathing quickened like he'd taken the stairs.

He stepped out on the fourth floor, the felony division of the district attorney's office. He forced enough air through his diaphragm to tell the receptionist behind the glass that he was the attorney for Marilyn Ramirez and he was there to look at the file. When he said Marilyn's name, the receptionist startled and excitedly punched numbers into her office phone too hard, and then she told her mouthpiece about Larry in a loud whisper.

Larry expected it. Last night he watched the local television stations' nightly Marilyn coverage from his pathetic, lonely hotel suite at ten.

"And we start tonight," said a middle-aged white man in a tie and navy jacket on the television, with channel 12 graphics behind him, "with the latest on Marilyn Ramirez, who is charged with two counts of attempted capital murder. We go to Sylvia Matthews outside the jail where Miss Ramirez is being held."

"Thank you, Bill," she said, speaking from the television, with the familiar jail behind her in the dark. She was a thirties-looking Hispanic with glued-down big hair and a red business suit jacket that every television reporter on the street owned. "I'm standing outside the Harris County Jail. Inside"—she held it for a second trying to be dramatic—"Marilyn Ramirez remains without bond. She was charged with two counts of attempted capital murder, along with two men, for allegedly attempting to shoot Ava Stonek, a well-known socialite in Houston. She was arrested three days ago after…"

She admitted to Larry she knew those guys, but the police didn't know that—at least they were not sure enough to write it down anywhere. If they had, Wiley or Miller would have a copy of it, and it would have been in the multisectioned file he had. Larry didn't know how, but they were good at getting police reports. Not even Jimenez or Bawany could identify Marilyn.

"However, Detective O. C. Simms…"—that name jerked Larry back to the report—"who is leading the investigation, continues to refuse to reveal what the police believe the motivation was, whether it was robbery or perhaps…"

"These reporters really are idiots," Larry thought.

"Sylvia," the news anchor said, "is there any word if the police believe any more people were involved?"

"No, Bill, when I asked Detective Simms if any more arrests were expected, he'd only say, 'No comment.' He also refused to speculate on Miss Ramirez's motive at this time."

"The investigation is still in process," said the head of a man with dark hair and gray sideburns on the screen. In the background it was daylight and there was no jail; it was obviously recorded at another time and place. Underneath his talking head, "Detective O. C. Simms, Houston Police Dept." was posted.

"Are any more arrests expected?" Sylvia asked from offscreen.

Simms's nose was long and pointed, and he had a mustache too small for his big head. He rumpled his mustache and answered, "No, I have no comment on that issue at this juncture. Our investigation will proceed with an analysis of the evidence available."

Sylvia appeared on the screen in front of the dark jail again. "Detective Simms would make no further comment, but other sources within the investigation hint that the police believe they haven't answered all the questions yet."

"Sylvia, is there any word how the victim, Mrs. Stonek, is doing?"

"She has recovered from the fall when her horse was shot to death, and she is currently at an undisclosed location…"

Lar stood next to Larry waiting for someone from behind the glass wall and excited receptionist to come get them, and sudden fear brought Larry back to reality. Panic burned through him, not because of what he knew he didn't know, but what he didn't dream of yet. What details should he watch for in the file? What arrest mistakes did the police make that he didn't even know were mistakes? What rules of court would he miss because he didn't know shit? Ms. Wiley couldn't think of everything. Lar grew stronger.

His pocket vibrated—his ringer was off—and he checked his phone. Ulm's office.

*"He's making sure you do as you're told,"* Lar said. It was best to ignore Lar. If Larry started responding, even thinking a response or acknowledging Lar's presence, it just all got worse. The phone popped with the notice of a new voice mail. *"How are you going to know what you're looking at?"* Lar said.

"Don't think," Larry told himself.

*"She can't save you. You can't be with her all the time."*

The panic burned like acid dumped in his stomach.

*"Murderers don't save people."*

The acid erupted, but he held it.

*"Especially not dumbasses."*

Two men in wrinkled white business shirts and ties walked down the long hall of offices behind the glass toward Larry. Quietly talking to each other, they both watched him as they walked, and one was familiar. The familiar one opened the side door, stuck out his hand to shake Larry's, and said, "Hey, Larry, remember me?" It was Chris Johnson, the Waller County Assistant District Attorney from the Bain case. Johnson was slightly taller than Larry and twenty years younger. He spoke and moved like a rodeo cowboy, but he was as sharp as any attorney Larry had ever met—anywhere.

"Hey, Chris Johnson. How are you doing? What are you doing here?"

"I work here now. You're not the only one that got famous out of the Bain case. Reid offered me a deal, so I came over." Reid was the elected DA in Harris County, which covered most of Houston.

"Really? Congratulations."

"Come on back, Larry." Johnson led him down the hall while they spoke. "Are you going to be the Ramirez attorney?" Johnson by mere chance had been assigned the unimportant Bain misdemeanor. He and Larry had a few very intense clashes. Larry demanded Bain be put in the

Federal Witness Protection Program over Johnson's venomous objections. When the press found out about it and that it involved Snow, there were more reporters in Waller for the hearings than citizens in the town. Not only were Bain's and Larry's faces on TV every night, but Johnson's, too, at least until Bain was found with a bullet in his head and the gun by his side.

The lazy police ruled it a suicide, and the media went on to other subjects one minute later. Larry went to jail charged with leaving the scene of an automobile accident, and after he was released checked himself into a psychiatric hospital. Bain's poor, old, brokenhearted mother was left to bury her only beloved son alone while tourists snapped pictures.

Larry never pretended to be any kind of trial attorney, and he knew Johnson wouldn't believe it if he did. "So, Chris, are you assigned the case?" he asked.

"Matter of fact, I am," he said with a short laugh. Chris showed Larry to an empty office where defense attorneys read the state's files, and an older, heavy woman in a gray suit brought the file.

"So, are you?" Chris asked. Chris stood up and stepped toward the door.

Larry kept the file closed, waiting for Chris to leave. "Am I what?"

"Don't play with me, now."

"I'm starting out. There'll be someone else for trial."

As he left, Chris said, "I'm sure he'll kick my ass." And he shut the door.

Larry checked the writing on the outside of the way, way too thin file considering the charges. Among the filled-in blanks, it showed the charges, bond denial, and that she'd never been arrested before. Inside the file, there was a police statement about when she was arrested, the charge papers of two attempted capital murders, and the bond denial paper—nothing else.

The entire police investigation was missing, and that meant they weren't finished.

Larry left the file and wandered down the hall to the office with Johnson's name on the outside of an opened door. "Hey, Chris," he said as he looked in at Johnson studying his computer at his desk, "where the hell's the rest of the file?" The one thing Larry could do well was act like he didn't know something.

Chris clicked off his screen and smiled from his chair. "Now you want to talk to me." He'd waited for Larry to come ask him about it.

"Nah, not today."

"Well, my heart's broken," Johnson drawled slowly. "Simms is not finished puttin' the pieces together that your lady's scattered everywhere." Chris twisted his head once. "She's a bad cat."

"Then I'm going to go visit Simms."

"That's your punishment," Chris said with false apathy.

# CHAPTER 7

There were not many perfect autumn days like this one in Houston, where it's mainly monsoon season, so Larry walked out of the district attorney's building to enjoy the weather on his way to the new METRORail. Houston had not had a real rail system like New York or Chicago since before World War I, and it barely did now, but it was a great part of the revitalized downtown. Marilyn's jail cell was just one block from the DA's office, and he felt her beckon to him. He longed to answer, though he knew he shouldn't want it. The new buildings, clean sidewalks, and other professionals rushing past Larry calmed him. He stepped on the train with other passengers, but he was alone, at least in his own mind. As the train passed through downtown, he called Diane to ask how the kids were, but she was too busy to talk.

He had four messages from Wiley and Miller—the one from Miller was the first time Larry had ever noticed his voice—and one from David— all worried for different reasons about what he was going to do next.

Though they had never met, Detective O. C. Simms greeted Larry with a big grin and a cheerful, "Nice to see you." He was tall, about fifty, and shaped like a bowling pin. He had a little untrimmed mustache, and when he got up and rushed to shake Larry's hand, he moved in a goofy, stiff way, like a broken robot. His expensive suit looked cheap because it was tailored to pull his pants over his stomach.

They met in Simms's office on the eleventh floor of the police building. His office was a combination of civil servant and expensive touches. The metal walls were decorated, and the steel desk was flanked with expensive chairs and topped with a designer lamp. There were two old pizza boxes with slices still in them in the trash can, and another by the lamp on the coffee table with one dull-looking slice dried out, with its edges curled up on top of the lid. Their smell lingered.

"You're Marilyn Ramirez's attorney? Ya gonna let me talk to her? You should let me talk to her; I know what's goin' on," Simms said quickly, not waiting for an answer or breath.

Larry sat down across from him. Simms had a disassembled black pistol—it looked like a semiautomatic—lying on his desk, and what at a glance appeared to be a car part schematic on his computer screen. "I just came to see your file," Larry finally interrupted.

Simms crunched down into his chair and picked up three parts of the gun, turned them over in his hands, and began snapping them together while he laughed. "Not likely. You can see the DA's file when he gets it. I'm not giving you shit." He looked hard at Larry. "I'm not buying what she's selling."

Larry was numb from how many times he was forced to hear Texas country expressions.

"You came to find out what she's told me." Simms continued to rush and snap together pieces. "She hasn't told me anything. This ain't her first rodeo."

"Detective Simms, my client has never been arrested before." Larry was grateful for the minions' research; at least he knew the facts.

Simms laughed, put his parts down hard on his desk, and started for the door. "Coffee? Come on," he said, but he left without waiting for Larry's answer.

Larry followed him to a dirty little kitchen that reeked of burned coffee. Simms handed him a Styrofoam cup. "Here, fix it like you like it." Simms stood close, not aggressively, but studying Larry. He hovered half a foot taller, "Say, you were Brian Bain's attorney, weren't you?"

Larry retreated to the counter and poured his coffee in a lump into his cup. He could hear phones ringing and police talking in the surrounding spaces, and he mumbled, "Yeah."

Simms studied Larry's face a second more, took a drink, and started walking back to his office. "It's rather a shame how that worked out. You know, I've got that file in my office. I never believed he killed himself."

*"I told you. I told you. You hid in that hellhole pretending you were getting over me, and I told you then that Bain didn't kill himself. He was too afraid of his own shadow. He was too scared to do it. You were more likely to kill him than he was to kill himself."*

Larry twitched and sat back down in Simms's office. Lar stood behind Larry and cleared his throat.

"What happened to you?" Simms asked from his own seat, relaxed and sitting back.

"I had some trouble; I got sick."

"I know. Why?"

"I thought they closed the file?"

"They did. I didn't. I can smell it. It doesn't smell like suicide."

*"It smells like death,"* Lar said.

"I'm really glad to hear that, Detective. I thought everyone forgot about that poor boy and his mother."

Detective Simms pulled a thick, dirty file from inside a side drawer of his desk and slapped it down. "Here it is. Closed and forgotten."

"Anything I can do to get it reopened?" Larry asked.

"I don't know yet, but thanks. I'll call if I have any questions."

"Now, how about Ramirez?" asked Larry.

"I'm not telling you anything on that, except I'm still in the middle of my investigation. You'll have to get your information on that from Johnson, but you're an OK guy. Look..." They both stood up and walked to the office door. "I may want to talk to you in a few days about it; let's just leave it at that." Simms walked Larry to the elevator, and they said good-bye.

As he walked back out in the bright sunlight to the Metrorail to report to Marilyn and Ulm, Larry now knew that Simms was after someone else who he suspected helped Marilyn try to murder Mrs. Stonek. And Simms must think this nefarious person was important enough to Marilyn that he could turn them against each other, which was why he wanted to talk to Larry "in a few days." He'd have to confront Marilyn about this person.

It shouldn't be a problem; his client wasn't anything other than average. She was pretty once, but not especially, and she wasn't particularly smart either, or she wouldn't have gotten herself in this mess. How was Simms going to find time to investigate the closed Bain suicide while working this case, along with whatever projects his desk and computer screen indicated? Larry was glad Simms thought he had time to reopen Bain, so Brian could get justice and so Simms wouldn't have as much time to investigate Marilyn—but he doubted Simms would really do it.

As he walked through the jail to the box, he thought how ridiculous his lying client looked in her obvious attempts to coax him to her. She clearly thought she was successful, and she'd be very surprised when he told her what he'd discovered and that he was quitting. Then, as he entered the box, he was angry that she thought she could so easily manipulate him—she underestimated him.

Lar scratched his way forward, twitching to the front of Larry's consciousness. *"Good. I'm happy. I'm glad you've kept this bitch. This is it. This is how I'll win."*

What was Lar saying? He had just decided to quit; he was sure he'd just thought that. Larry sat surrounded by the echoing boom of distant doors and angry, yelling, muffled voices beyond the walls bearing onto him and waited for her.

*"Where's Diane? Not so important since you met this bitch, is she? You think you're so superior, and she's just a dud? Last time you met with her fifteen minutes, and you rolled over like a Chihuahua."*

When Larry first saw Lar, he was just a shadow, a dark man. Later he saw Lar had black eyes and a broken nose. In the last few days, Lar had gained a distinct body, down to pockmarked cheeks, old jeans, blue work shirt with some garage name on the pocket, and a fake leather jacket.

Larry felt his chair vibrate when a heavy door very close slammed shut. The crashing sound echoed through the steel all around him, and it momentarily jarred him out of his thoughts. He surreptitiously looked around—maybe Marilyn was coming.

"*I'm in control,*" Lar said, but he wasn't. As long as Larry remembered that Lar wasn't real, Larry believed he could hold Lar off. "*Bull, you're weak. This bitch's my key.*"

Now that Larry saw Lar, he must not argue with him, fight with him, never deal with him like he was real, because when Larry did, he stepped into Lar's world. Larry must ignore him. In Lar's world, Larry lost control of his car in the middle of the night while kidnapping his own children because Diane was trying to murder them all. In his world, believing Diane a murderer was perfectly rational. That's why even as Lar appeared clearer and more alive, as Larry heard him more often when he was scared or nervous, Larry must not recognize him.

"Larry?" Marilyn was sitting directly in front of Larry, and her smiling face seemed to glow. "I'm so happy to see you. I knew you'd be here for me."

"How are you this morning?"

"It's cold. And it's smelly." She shivered and wrinkled her nose, and Larry cursed himself for thinking it was cute. Before Marilyn, he'd never been in the women's blocks before, but that smell was familiar: body odor magnified with urine, all washed over with extremely diluted Clorox. He needed to be on guard; he couldn't slide down that slope again.

"*She does have just a hint of snake legs, ready to wrap around a guy, the way she sits there.*"

"You look rested. You must be able to sleep in here."

His comment made her blush. How does a forty-year-old woman sitting in jail manage to do that?

"*I'll tell you; she's a fucking con artist.*"

She leaned onto the desk, her loose orange overalls with "PRISONER" printed on them drooped, and the dirty white undershirt exposed her milky long neck. She kept her hair back to ensure she exposed her neck. He remembered to breathe and then swallow.

"Larry?"

He woke up. "Yes."

"Did you find out anything?"

"Huh?"

*"Yeah, that Simms's going to freaking hang your ass."*

"Yes, Simms isn't finished," Larry said.

She leaned back, her body relaxed. Larry watched Lar move until he stood right behind her, silently laughing.

"You mean Detective Simms?" she said.

As he looked back from Lar to Marilyn, Larry noticed her looking him in the eyes. "Yes," he said.

"He thinks I'm some supermastermind." Her tone was mocking, but her posture showed she was proud of it.

*"If you were a master, you wouldn't be in jail, you stupid bitch."*

"Well, she's not then," Larry thought, "so don't worry about it."

*"You don't have a brain at all anymore; don't get me wrong—I like it—but don't act like you're superior."*

"I'm not," Larry responded, "and nothing's wrong with my brain; I'm just trying to talk to my client. Please go away."

"Larry?" she said as she looked back into his eyes.

"Yes?"

"What did he say?"

"Who?" he thought. Then he said, "Nothing, but what I got from him is that there's someone else. Someone else close to you that they're after." He was telling her as much as he knew, hoping to ingratiate himself. "And in a couple of days, he thinks he'll have them, and he's going to try to get you to roll over on each other." He hadn't reported that last part to the minions.

"Does that happen often?" she asked, wholly innocent of this nasty system.

"All the time." Larry acted experienced. "Every time. People are stupid."

*"Dude, it's a guy."* Lar strung out the last word. *"Look at her. It's a guy, and he won't roll over anymore than you would right now, but she will, she will. She'd sell your soul for a dollar."*

Larry blinked, and Marilyn said, "What's the matter, Larry?" She leaned toward him, her lips wet. He could feel her breath. There was a spotlight on her face, he thought. "Tell me."

"It's nothing." He blinked Lar away for a moment and said, "I can't get anything from the DA. You'll have to wait until we hear from the police."

"I know you; you're not leaving me, Larry, are you? I need you."

Larry's head buzzed. "No, I'm not leaving you. I'll keep checking with Simms. He's a nice enough guy. I might be able to get a little more out of him."

"Larry, I know you can't get me out of here right now, can you?"

"No, there's no way right now with the police investigation where it is."

"Yeah, I heard the judge say I was a flight risk when he denied bail before you were helping me. I can't get in contact with the person that's supposed to pick up my mail and take care of my cat. Could you call my friend and just make sure he knows that I need him to do it?"

"Call your friend?" Larry didn't want to do it.

"You won't have to remember anything; just call and tell him to do what I asked."

"What'd you ask?"

"Well, when I knew the police were trying to blame me for this, I asked him to take care of my cat and stuff—no big deal—so I just need to know that he's doing it."

Larry couldn't think of why he shouldn't do this. The cat could die—it was just a cat—but even now in her glowing presence, he didn't quite trust her.

"So would you call him for me?"

"Sure."

"*Dumbass.*"

# CHAPTER 8

From a twentieth-floor window, Ava looked out on the green canopy and fountains of Hermann Park and Rice University. To her right she saw the museum district, and beyond that the dark geometric lines of downtown Houston outlined in a heat haze. Her envious friends told her it was like an apartment in Manhattan overlooking Central Park, but she preferred to think of it as Fort Knox. She and Don had owned this place for a while, but she had resisted moving from her home. After strange men attacked her shooting guns on two occasions, Don finally convinced her it was safer here. After all, she escaped only because the shooters were idiots.

Thank God the men that attacked her left tracks like children running through fresh snow. The police arrested both before they could change clothes, and both heaved all they knew about their accomplice. The trouble was that the two defendants couldn't identify who their accomplice was. Ava and the police knew who it was—to Ava's ultimate humiliation, her husband's whore. The police detective told her the trouble was proof.

The defendants described a woman with different hair color and name, like switching a name or putting on a cheap wig was hard. Ava watched the recording of that tramp, handcuffed, shoved into the police car repeatedly. It was butter.

Don's sorry now, the whore's in jail and she's surely ready to say anything to save herself, and that ridiculous detective keeps questioning Don about what he knew and when he knew it, like he was Nixon. Detective Simms, she remembered as she sat on the couch with her view and sipped her green tea. More of a caricature of a detective than what she had perceived as a police detective. When he asked her questions, all she could think about were those strange trousers he pulled up to his stomach. Why would a man do that?

Of course, it scared her when that man chased her. And then that monster murdered her precious Joe; that was worse than killing her. But the embarrassment of constant television reports of the attacks, the whore's arrest, Don charged as an accomplice by the police and after posting bail walking out of the police station protected by a phalanx of attorneys was more than she could endure. They moved here, on the twentieth floor of this modern castle, so she'd be safe from attackers and isolated from her humiliation.

Not that Ava's safety was in danger anymore since that woman was stuck in jail and not getting out, but it helped her hide from her dear friends' subtle questions and those rude reporters. Was there ever anything more embarrassing than five television trucks parked on her secluded street in front of her home with their satellite dishes extended up fifty-foot poles? She knew what the neighbors thought, and she knew what her best friends said.

"Dumbass lawyer." Michael Williams was nineteen years old, and he survived because he was bigger and he picked the right gang. He made good money from pussies. He'd picked up a few cuts, but the big wound on his neck was good for business.

When that white guy called his phone, he didn't answer it; he never answered it, just like Miss Donna had told him. He just listened to the dumbass message. The fucker said that Miss Ramirez had been arrested, but that she wanted him to go ahead with the plan to take care of her cat, and she'd pay him any costs when she got out. Mike needed the money; ice cost, and that fucking money she gave him was gone. She told him before when she gave him the phone, a picture, two guns, five hundred dollars, and a rock to get high—that was nice—that he might get a message like that if she got arrested, and to erase the message and destroy the phone afterward. It was a good phone with more time on it, so he kept it. Fuck her.

Miss Ramirez wasn't the name she told him. Michael called her Miss Donna, but she'd told him it might be another name. That's cool; he'd done that. She had more scams than he did, but he didn't give a shit; he just wanted the rest of his money. She told him where that bitch would be hiding if he got the call and that he'd need to watch out for security, but he wasn't afraid of a couple of lazy pigs that just walked around. She said he could slip in the back of the garage and get her there.

Michael snuck into the garage three times and waited. That part was easy; he sat down on the clean floor behind a big Mercedes or a little Porsche. He liked the red Porsche the best, where he could see people come out or park. The only problem was the valets, but they were in such a hurry they didn't see anything. Twice he went by himself, but it was boring so he left and got high. The third time he was already high and his friend wouldn't loan him his car, so Michael made the guy take him. They stayed until a bunch of men in white uniforms came in to sweep out the garage, which was strange because it was already cleaner than anywhere Michael had ever lived.

Now, as he sat there waiting for the fourth time, he knew he didn't have any more damn time. He'd spent all his fucking money, and he needed ice. He'd already whored for credit and he'd traded one of the guns, so the fucking bitch had to die today no matter how long he had to wait. He'd made someone in the house where he woke up take him to the garage; it must have been sometime in the afternoon because the sun was high and it was so damn hot, but Michael wasn't sure and didn't care. He squatted down in his regular hiding place with his gun down between his legs. He hurt, and as he sat in the cool, dark shadows of the corner of the garage smoking, he was so depressed he thought of using the gun on himself. She was never going to come out; he didn't know why he ever thought he could just wait out here and she'd just walk up like a pig.

After Ava ate lunch, she dressed to go to the club to work out, run, and have a couple of martinis. At first, she was afraid to leave her fortress, but Don urged her to not lock herself in a prison now that it was safe, so every day she drove to her club, which had its own guards. She had her maid pack a change of clothes so she could shower and change before she met her friends. The first time she left, even leaving the building terrified her, and she ran to her car when the valet drove it around to the front. She quickly regained her confidence, and she found the courage to walk through the protected garage to her car on the basement floor, the privileged closest parking spot among the privileged spots.

Michael heard the elevator door bing as it opened, and he looked up to check the face, knowing that just like every other time, it wouldn't be her—just failure. It would never be her; he had no hope. There was no way he'd get that fucking money, the lying Miss Donna would never get out of jail anyway, and how would he find her to collect if she did? He didn't know shit about her, except she was in jail right now. She found him. She contacted him, gave him his shit. He didn't even have her fucking number, so how was he going to find her if she didn't call him?

He was such a dumbass, he never thought of this shit until he was crouched in the shadows with this fucking gun between his legs; he should just pull the fucking trigger now, and he's waiting on some bitch to show up that never will. What a stupid, fucking dumbass, but he checked the face. An old blond lady. It's her, he thought he remembered; it's got to be her—it's her.

Michael jumped up, put his shaking finger on the trigger as he pulled the gun up, and walked quickly as he wound through the cars to catch her, quietly; he couldn't breathe, and he skipped, he tried to move so fast. She didn't see him yet, and then when he popped out from between two cars, she caught him in the corner of her eyes, dropped her purse and bag, and ran. Michael broke into his hardest run and closed on her instantly. It seemed to Michael like she hardly moved, like she ran in place.

She twisted to face him as he caught her, her face in terror and her hand outstretched like she could hold him away, like that'd do any good. She looked like she was trying to scream, but nothing came out of her mouth except some funny gravel sound. Michael pointed the gun and fired, and the explosive sound hit him as hard as the bullet hit her in her gut, and her blood splattered his jeans. How was he going to get that shit off?

She smashed to the floor, and the booming sound of the shot echoed through Michael's ears over and over. He panicked. He knew those fat pigs that stayed upstairs eating all the time or the running valets heard it, so he ran. He ran through the cars, trying to breathe, and he regretted not putting another bullet in her head while she lay on the floor in a growing lake of the same red goo that was all over his jeans. That bitch's blood was in his mouth, all salty and metal-like, and then he stopped thinking and just ran.

Ava wondered why she didn't hurt more. She lay still like she'd been thrown into wet cement and then it dried. She couldn't move, didn't want to; she didn't know if she was even breathing. She tried to make herself breathe, the way you can take a conscious breath, but she couldn't, or at least she couldn't tell whether she had.

The warm floor under her grew redder, but the floor of the garage wasn't red, and she wondered what that was, and then it struck her that she was being warmed by her own blood. If she was bleeding, she should get up and get help, but she didn't, didn't try, and she didn't know why, and then she didn't care. She just rested.

She must not be awake—that must be why she wouldn't try to get up and save herself. And then she realized she must be dead, and the horror and grief swept her into numb surrender. She was overwhelmed with terror, her whole life gone, but she didn't cry out or even make a sound; she just lay there motionless, with no expression even of the unfairness of it, the end of everything, the end of her.

# CHAPTER 9

The bloodstained corpse laid in the corner of the room. Red covered the floor, one wall, and Bain's body. The next picture was a close-up of the large bullet hole in the side of his head. Simms liked this picture.

"Once in a while, even idiots get something right," he said to himself. He knew what a .38 hole looked like when the gun was jammed next to the head, and he knew it didn't look like Bain's head. This shot was from three, three and a half feet. Bain couldn't have shot himself. But the file said the investigating detective concluded it was suicide. The .38 was found in Bain's hand. Lazy. Malfeasance. Normal.

Simms completed reading the old Bain file, dirty and dusty from its time in storage boxes, and closed it. It was typical, sloppy work. A detective sees an easy possible solution that offers him a chance to close another case with less paperwork, and he takes it. God forbid he have to reason or, worse, research something, and the science labs that work alongside of the detectives had been such a disgrace for so long that the appellate courts even acknowledged it, which in Texas was the same as hell freezing. Since Bain's suicide was obviously murder, everyone at the labs had been fired. Hundreds of cases were reversed because of the incompetent detectives and their science lab coconspirators. "Criminal negligence," Simms thought. And so he expected to find something wrong with every old file he opened. It was too easy, too simple, too convenient that in the middle of a scandal destroying Washington, the only witness was found with a bullet in his head and the gun in his dead hand.

Simms told the twenty-fifth floor then, but they wouldn't let him on the case. He dealt with that all the time—resistance. The good ole boys in the department thought Simms was a know-it-all, and compared to them, he was. Some of the other detectives got confused and thought they were the same because they all went to Texas A&M, but the difference was that they were lazy and stupid and bit the hook on obvious; they were not the same, and they learned it quickly. O. C. Simms was sure he knew the right wine with any dish, how to change the motor on a professional-grade grass edger, and what the bullet hole should look like when a man rams a .38 against his head, and it was not like what he was looking at.

He'd intended to review the Bain file sooner, but he'd been too busy. After hell froze and the twenty-fifth floor panicked, he was assigned all the big cases—and none were as big to the public as the Ramirez case. When Bain's old attorney showed up representing Ramirez, Simms remembered he wanted to reexamine Bain, and he needed more than another screwup by the detectives and science labs before he went upstairs.

The city purchased a twenty-six-floor high-rise in 1989, when Houston's collapsed economy left empty office buildings all over town, and rebuilt it into a police headquarters out of an Orwellian novel. The tall walls and over-size square design dwarfed the individual as it was approached. It seemed without color, like a black-and-white picture of itself, and its outdated fluorescent lighting made weird moving shadows all around.

Among many other traits they hated about Simms, the twenty-fifth floor despised it when he requested to open old, solved cases. The twenty-sixth floor never even knew it, of course; it was occupied by political appointees. Simms thought of it as occupied because they surely didn't work. The real command worked one floor below them, and just like in police departments all over the world, they were buried in whatever crimes they were dealing with, all of it desperately urgent to the complaining victims. No one wanted more work.

When the labs were revealed as incompetent, hundreds of prisoners were bonded out of the state prisons in Huntsville and new trials set. The Houston Police Department could not endure reopening a political scandal because of more of its own malfeasance. Simms would need more, and he thought he'd start with Bain's attorney.

Before he could call Lamb, he got a call from a crime scene and was told Ava Stonek had been attacked again, and this time she'd been shot.

When Simms pulled up in a car at the basement of the blue high-rise, officers were running around and yellow tape stretched everywhere. Simms knew this building—it was only five years old, an art piece of architectural design and interior original modern art, and constructed so poorly that the developer, contractor, and unit owners were all suing one another.

Ava Stonek was already at the hospital when Simms walked under the tape. Detectives were in groupings questioning possible witnesses and taking pictures. A young uniform rushed up to him with a tablet and said, "Sir, an unknown assailant or assailants shot Ava Stonek one time in the abdomen, and then fled the scene. There are no known witnesses at this time."

Simms thought, "These young guys—'at this time.' He's already trying to speak the way he thinks a detective speaks. What other time was it?"

"Robbery does not appear to be a motive at this time as Mrs. Stonek still wore her wedding ring and diamond watch, and her purse was not taken," the officer said.

"'At this time' again…stop using that phrase," he thought.

"No weapon was found at the scene." The officer wouldn't shut up. Not robbery—no shit.

"Do we have cars in surrounding streets yet? The shooter is probably still in the area. He may be walking around lost," Simms said.

"How do you know that, sir?"

"Because that's what the last two shooters did."

"Yes, sir. We have patrol cars on every street, but they haven't seen anyone yet."

"Well, stay with it. He's probably still wandering around."

The young man ran off to do as Simms ordered, and Simms stood in the cool basement looking down at a large, congealed red pool. It was a nice day, warm, and after he got something to eat, he was definitely calling that lawyer.

Larry changed cell phone numbers soon after he took Marilyn's case; he had to. Reporters found his old number, and his phone never stopped—they wanted comments or interviews. Authors called wanting to ghostwrite a book about the case, and agents called with ideas. Then there were the old friends he could barely remember offering encouragement and suggestions. The only people he gave his new number to were his kids, Diane, and the office. He had the store block other IDs when he bought the phone. But Ulm acquired it immediately; he wanted his updates.

Larry knew Stonek was shot in a garage and the police would blame Marilyn, though he didn't see how they'd rationalize it. The jailers monitor all nonattorney communications prisoners like her have with the outside world. He warned her of it to make sure she didn't say anything to anyone that might be misinterpreted. If anything, the fact that Ava Stonek was shot again should exonerate Marilyn. Larry felt conflicted, condemning the police for their paranoid attitude about Marilyn. Simms was at least giving Bain's death another examination—it wasn't suicide.

His office called and told him Detective Simms wanted to come by the office, but Larry had her call back and say he'd drop by Police Headquarters instead. Larry expected the Simms call; Ulm's lackeys called him earlier on his new, secret line and warned him in single phrases that they were sure he could understand that the police would very soon want to talk to his client again. They reminded him that it appeared—they emphasized *appeared*—that his client gave the police nothing before Larry intervened, and that all the police currently had—and they emphasized the word *currently* so poor, stupid Larry understood properly—was the hysterical claims of Mrs. Stonek and some confused descriptions by the shooters.

Larry didn't worry about anyone tricking Marilyn anymore. No one was going to deceive her into saying anything she didn't intend to. He was crazy to stay on the case and he was humiliated by his own worshipful behavior every time he was in her presence, but he wasn't getting off the case and he couldn't choose not to go back to her. When he was away from her, he knew the truth—she really wasn't anything special; she really wasn't even that smart.

She may have gotten herself into the mess she was in out of some deluded belief that the police would never find out about her—her with her stupid wigs—and that Don Stonek would promptly marry her after his wife's murder. Larry now knew about Stonek's and Marilyn's affair. Miss Wiley and her legs e-mailed him a supplemental brief of known facts, but he'd heard it on channel 12 the day before. He doubted Marilyn, at least when he wasn't with her, but it didn't matter. He'd defend her whether or not she was guilty, but it greatly disturbed him that a woman he believed might have tried to kill another woman twice, maybe three times now, possessed him. He had to stop it, and he knew he'd thought that before, and he meant to test himself after he met with Simms. He couldn't stay away from her anyway.

Simms stood at the door of his office, his pants pulled up over his stomach and held there with braces, wearing a white business shirt and yellow tie, with a smile on his too-big head like he was meeting with a good friend—or someone with good news. Larry was surprised at it as he walked up because he'd begun to believe Simms was going to try to bully him into agreeing to allow Simms to further question Marilyn. Larry didn't know what was going to happen if Legs's e-mail memos didn't predict it; he'd never been in a murder case or even walked through floors of the police headquarters every day to talk to detectives about a shooting. It was surreal.

"Mr. Lamb, thank you for coming over so quickly," Simms said, shaking Larry's hand too hard and showing him a chair as he sat down behind his desk.

"It really wasn't quick. It's almost six o'clock. Don't you ever go home?" Larry said as he sat on the edge of the chair.

"Yeah, yeah. Can I get you some coffee?"

"No, it's too late. I just want to get out of here and go have dinner."

"I'm sorry. It's obviously been a wild day; after the shooting and some other stuff, I just thought we needed to talk. I thought you might give me some help."

Help? What type of help did Simms think Larry would give him? First, Larry is Simms's best friend, and then he wants help. Larry's confusion produced Lar sitting on the credenza behind Simms. He didn't say anything; he just lounged, enjoying himself. Larry noticed what he wore again and reconciled that this new, stronger, more developed Lar was not fading away.

"I need to talk to your client again," Simms said.

Larry couldn't remember what they were talking about before Simms said that, but guessed. "You know it's not going to happen."

"I know she was behind this shooting, too, Larry. You better start giving me something before we catch this last idiot. When we do, and you know we will because she only tricks stupid shits into doing her dirty work, I'm going to hang her."

*"How you think she did it?"* Lar wondered.

"You don't know she did," Larry thought, and then he said, "How could she do it from jail? You'd know."

Simms waited a minute after Larry's answer, and then he said, "I'll figure it out. Those other two morons described her to a T"—Simms emphasized—"and if Mrs. Stonek dies, I'll execute her."

"You don't have anything, Simms, and you know it, or else you wouldn't be so excited about number three, and yes, I need coffee if I'm not going to have dinner anytime soon."

*"I don't think she planned it completely ahead of getting arrested."* Lar pretended to think out loud.

"I will have number three. I caught those other two after just a few hours."

*"She's too stupid to plan that far ahead. In her first two tries…"*

"I can't help you tonight," Larry said. "Where's my coffee?"

Simms left the office, and Lar slid off the credenza and leaned against it, crossing his arms. *"She had help, or got a message out to her latest dumb fuck."*

"You shouldn't put me off. The first…" Simms said as he came back and handed Larry his cup.

Larry was ready for this speech. Legs's fifteenth e-mail of the day predicted it, even predicted the next sentence would be a blatant attempt to create a panic rush. The lack of subtlety implied Simms wasn't impressed with Larry's intelligence.

"…one that turns gets the deal."

"Not tonight." Larry took a sip.

*"Yeah, that bitch might not be dead yet. Let's wait and see how many more shots it takes."*

Detective Simms relaxed, slapped the file shut, and slid another old manila folder on top of it.

*"She's smart enough to get the word out; maybe she picked someone a little smarter this time to do the job,"* Lar said.

"I need to ask you something else, too. Look at this stuff," Simms said as he handed papers over. "It's Bain. We don't have much on his death—nothing really, they closed it so fast."

Larry stopped reaching for it.

"Don't worry; I took the pictures out. It's just that I know it couldn't be a suicide, and I'm hoping to get something from you to help me."

Larry opened the file, and the papers were a police form describing how the body was found, an autopsy, and witness statements from Larry and Bain's mother. "The final page," Simms said as Larry turned to it, "concludes that Brian Bain died of a self-inflicted gunshot."

It was nothing new, and Larry said, "I'd like to help you, Detective, on this, I really would, but there's nothing in here. What can I tell you?"

"What do you think happened?"

"You know what I think? Somebody killed him to shut him up, and it worked."

Simms was aggravated and said, "Let's start this way. Tell me about the last time you saw him. What'd he say? Did he mention anybody that he thought might hurt him?"

"Yeah, you know, there were a lot of men that wanted him quiet—Snow for one."

"Snow's dead," Simms said.

"I don't believe it. Brian didn't either."

Simms pretended to look through the file to check that, and then he said, "I don't see anywhere in here where you said anything about that. Your statement just says that you were representing Bain on an exposure case."

"It wasn't exposure, and I was limited about what I could say at the time. I had attorney-client confidences."

"You don't now."

"No, I don't. Maybe I do. I think I'm helping Brian more now by helping you if you're reopening his murder."

"Suicide right now."

"It's always been murder to me."

"I think it is, too, but I need help."

*"Blah, blah, blah—don't help this motherfucker. If you start helping this piece of shit, you're liable to expose Marilyn,"* Lar yelled.

"Since when are you concerned about Marilyn?" thought Larry.

*"Me. I'm killing your ass. I don't need any help from him,"* Lar said as he nodded toward Simms.

Larry breathed, then he took several robotic breaths unnoticeable to anyone outside his mind to allow himself to think again, and then he said, "Brian was hiding. His mom was giving him money. I didn't even know where he was."

"You didn't ask him?"

"As you intimated in the past, you know what state I was in. My—" Larry stopped himself, or Lar stopped him. Larry intended to say that he was so over his head and bewildered about what to do next, he was so angry that he was stuck in the middle of it, that he was busy chasing his wife and her murderous boyfriend, waiting for them outside hotels and crashing cars fleeing from them, that he was not able to think clearly. No, he was just going to say he was losing his mind, but he shouldn't have said that either, so Lar was right for stopping him. Lar took charge and stopped him—he knew it—but then he shivered at the sudden realization that Lar had the power to stop him from saying something. When did that start? Was this the first time it happened, or was it just the first time Larry noticed it?

"So you didn't know where he was hiding?" Simms asked.

"No idea."

"You didn't know he was at the house he was found in?"

"No, I guess only his mom knew," Larry said, and then added, "I guess she did. He had to tell someone else. I don't remember."

*"Good job."* Lar smiled.

"Well"—Simms looked off as if he was frustrated, and then back at Lamb—"let's try it like this. Did you talk to him on the day he died?"

"I think so. I don't know. What's my statement say?"

"It says you talked to him the last couple of days before his death."

*"They've already checked it, man."*

"No. Did they check Brian's phone?" Larry asked.

"They didn't find it; just mentioned it wasn't located at the scene."

"And didn't they think that was a little funny?"

"Of course not."

Acid burned Larry's stomach, and he gave more power to Lar. The police didn't care Brian lay dead with a hole in his head; it just solved a problem.

"I know Bain thought Snow wanted to get rid of him, but that's not enough. Can you give me any name, description of someone following him, anything? Can I look through your file?" Simms said.

Larry knew he legally might resist Simms getting his client's file, but he wanted to help. "Sure; let me find it."

# CHAPTER 10

**"D**iane?" Larry called her after he left Simms's office. Even a voice was better than eating a hotel hamburger alone.

"Is it too late to talk to the kids?" He knew it was, but he couldn't stop himself—didn't try.

"They're asleep. Do you want me to wake them up so you can talk to them?" Diane said.

He needed to talk to them—and her. He was sick. Sicker than he'd ever been before, even in the hospital, and like long ago, Diane sensed Larry needed them.

"No, I don't want you to wake them up. Just tell them Daddy called and that he loves them." "And I love you, too—if I'd just not destroyed us," he thought.

"I'll wake them up," she said.

"Thanks, but no. When they get up in the morning, have them call me."

"OK Larry."

"Diane?"

"Yes."

"Thank you so much."

Silence, and then she said, "How are you doing, Larry? What's wrong?"

"I'm just lonely tonight."

Silence again, and then, "Maybe it'd help if you started seeing a doctor again."

"It might." He didn't like saying no to her.

"What time are you coming to see the kids Friday?"

"Can I pick them up from school?"

"Yeah, Katie loves it when you surprise her at school."

"OK," Larry said.

"Bye, Larry."

"Bye." He wanted to say "I love you" but couldn't anymore. It was like some kind of divorce rule; once you're divorced, you're not allowed to tell your ex that anymore.

The next morning Miller waited for him in the tunnel as Larry walked to the jail. Miller was a young black man who wore fashionable glasses and a prep-school accent like an Ivy Leaguer wears a sweater tied around his neck.

"We've e-mailed you the latest on Johnson. He's presumably waiting on Simms. The tunnel to the jail is down this way." He pointed it out. "Don't forget..."

"Where's Legs?" Larry interrupted Miller's instructions as they walked underground to avoid the reporters.

"Legs? What Legs?"

"Wiley."

"Oh, huh, she does have nice legs. Today was my turn to meet you. Don't forget to leave the jail by the tunnel, too. You have a better chance of missing the gang of cameras waiting for you..."

Marilyn arrived almost as soon as Larry sat down. She looked just like he'd expect a woman to look if she lived in a jail—exhausted and dirty.

"I've been waiting on you, Larry." She sat down hard, sideways, and with her left shoulder blocking him.

Startled, he pulled his file out, opened to the notes section for this date, and wrote, "She already knows what I'm going to tell her." Then, to satisfy her, he said, "I didn't finish with Detective Simms until late. Too late to come here. He wants to talk to you again."

"I had nothing"—she spun around in her chair to face him and raised her voice—"nothing to do with her getting shot. I know you told him that." She then relaxed her body, forgiving him for making her wait.

"Of course, I did. I told him there was no way you could have had anything to do with it since you were locked in here and isolated from everyone."

"Exactly," she said, as if she was relieved he finally understood it.

"But he's convinced you did it, or got someone to do it, rather."

"Ol' Weird Pants—did you notice how he wears his pants? It's funny."

"I told him there's no way."

"I'm not talking to him; he scares me."

Larry doubted that. Marilyn was a mystery to him, like a burning flame the first time a child sees it. It dances and swirls, and the child wants to get closer to it and touch it.

"No, I'm not scared," she said, warm and forgiving. "I know you'll protect me."

No matter what his mother says, the child will touch it.

"My file sure is thick…" she said, leaning and looking at what Larry was reading. "Is that from the firm paying you to protect me?"

The child will touch it.

"How did she know that?" he wondered.

*"I'll tell you how, you stupid fuck; the damn name's on the inside of the file. She leans over half the table so you can get a better view of her titties; she can fucking read,"* Lar said.

"I thought you were gone," Larry thought.

*"Where am I going?"* Lar said. *"Paris?"*

"Larry?" she said.

"You read the name on the file."

"Of course—how else?" She laughed, and that made him feel better.

*"You stupid…"* Lar would not tolerate Larry relaxing.

"Are you OK, Larry?" She looked very concerned, and her warm tone helped Larry fight Lar.

"Yes, I'm fine…I'm just…worried…working hard—" he stuttered, "to protect you."

"I know you are, but you drift sometimes. What's wrong? Tell me." She studied him, then sat back, relaxed and open. "It's not important." She nodded at the file. "Do any of those files tell you I had to go to a hospital once to rest?"

"No, I didn't know." Larry was calm and feeling open, too, and Lar said nothing.

"I needed some rest, to get away from chaos for a little while, you understand, don't you?" She looked as if she worried he might judge her for it.

"Yes." Larry wanted to relieve her fears. "I do. I understand totally." He was excited, possibly knowing Marilyn's intimate secret, one Legs may not even know about.

"People always judge it when you have to do that. They label you, but you don't label me, do you?"

"No, no, I had to go rest once, too." Did he tell her that?

"Really, see, it's not about strong or weak; you're about the strongest man I know, and you needed to be."

"Rest wasn't really it, though." He didn't mind telling her a part of his truth; she'd suffered, too, and he rationalized that if he could get her to open up a little more, it could help him defend her. "I thought someone was following me," he confessed. "I was having trouble with my wife, and I thought she had a boyfriend and he was following me." That was way more than he intended, but she didn't act surprised or put-off, but rather, concerned and compassionate. He'd always distrusted these emotions—he was too cynical to even like them—but Marilyn cared.

"Larry," she said. He loved how she pronounced his name. "I'm so sorry. You know, I never did really get any rest there either—not really. I finally gave up and left."

"Me too—never." He'd never admitted that to anyone before; he hadn't intended to admit it now. The whole conversation felt incredible.

Marilyn changed looks, colors, expressions, like a chameleon; she was stern, medical almost. "You still see him, Larry." She stopped, analyzed and studied what she was seeing, calculating beyond Larry's impression of what was happening, in his face, in his body, in his reaction to what she said.

"You do." She saw it, and then she caught herself, changed herself again to a caring but determined friend. "I'm still tired, too, and worse now. The stresss…"—she strung out the s's as if she was just finishing the operating manual for Larry; it was complicated, and she wanted to get the manual right—"makes it worse. He's close now, isn't he?"

*"What the fuck?"* Lar screamed. Larry tried to smother him down, but Lar pushed out next to him, detailed down to dirty brown steel-toed work shoes and vodka breath. Lar's scream hit Larry in the face with spittle. The shock that he could smell and feel Lar made him dizzy.

He may have fainted. He was still sitting in the chair, but Marilyn stood over him holding him. He felt her soft hands touching his neck and face.

"Larry, are you OK?" The scent of her jail coveralls wasn't so bad. She had never touched him like this before. "I didn't mean to upset you."

"Thank you. I'm sorry; I'm fine."

The steel door slammed open, and an angry guard jumped in.

# CHAPTER 11

**"W**hat the hell is going on in here?" The fat guard grabbed Marilyn and threw her toward the door. Larry stared as Marilyn bounced off the concrete wall and the guard ripped her hands behind her back.

"No," he said as his mind rebooted. The guard shoved her to the floor with his knee in her back and handcuffed her. "No, deputy, stop. It's OK. Nothing happened."

As he lifted her back to her feet by her cuffs, the guard said, "Prisoners know they aren't allowed to cross the room or touch anyone. She's attacking you. I saw."

"No. I fainted." Larry looked at Marilyn's red face to confirm it, but she didn't act like she knew what Larry was talking about; she just sucked air.

Two female guards rushed in and pushed the man away from Marilyn, grabbed her on both sides, and led her to the door.

"You'll have to talk to the sergeant about that. She broke the law," the belly-heaving deputy said.

As she passed the hall window, Marilyn looked at Larry. She acted unhurt and gave him a knowing smile.

"That's…" Larry stopped speaking as he looked at the space Marilyn had just occupied. What did her look mean? Then, shaking, he said, "That's nonsense." He said as he looked back to the guard, "I fainted, and she kept me from cracking my head on the floor that you threw her against." He gathered himself as he stood and roared, "What I'm talking to him about is your brutality with a female prisoner."

The guard stomped out of the room and slammed the prisoner door. Stunned by Marilyn's look, Larry forgot about the sergeant and walked out the front door of the jail numb—"what does she know?" he wondered.

A pretty young woman with a channel 13 button on her chest yelled, "Did Ms. Ramirez hire the man to murder Mrs. Stonek?" as she shoved a big, black microphone into Larry's face. A burly man with a mobile television camera hiding his head chased her. Larry had forgotten to take the tunnel and stepped into a trap.

"Mr. Lamb, Mr. Lamb." He heard a man's voice yelling his name as a pack of panicked, screaming reporters and their accompanying cameras rushed at him. Seasoned among the pushers were older and lesser-dressed jostlers with little recorders and microphones—radio and print reporters. "Have the shooters made a deal with the prosecutors yet?" He turned himself sideways and tried to slip between crevices of the oncoming pack, but a shoulder attached to a camera the size of a rocket launcher blocked him and then shoved him back. Larry tried to look over the jumping reporters to get help from Miller, but he wasn't there. This was his mistake and he'd have to escape by himself. "Did you speak with Miss Ramirez?" Stupid question—why else would he be here? He pushed forward a step. "Will Miss Ramirez talk to the police?" He thought, "Why would I let her do that? Why would I tell you? You're all so lazy."

*"That one is cute though,"* Lar said.

Larry tried to take another step, but a skinny kid in a red sweater with a miniature recorder pushed between two television reporters and blocked his path.

*"Fucker,"* Lar said.

One of the reporters shouldered the kid back, and he fell.

"Excuse me," Larry said as the pack stepped over the kid who tried to stand. "Please let me pass." The rolling crowd of men, women, and cameras encircled him, each one trying to stick their microphone or recorder closer to Larry's mouth than the others.

"Has Miss Ramirez spoken to Don Stonek?" "How long has she been his mistress?" "If Mrs. Stonek dies, do you expect the DA to ask for the death penalty?"

*"Follow me,"* Lar said.

"No…no comment," Larry said.

Lar pushed him through the crowd, showing Larry how to avoid the scrawny kids trying to block him. They broke free, but the pack chased. The poorly dressed ones had the advantage and stayed closer for a moment. Big cameras weren't as mobile. Larry followed Lar to the corner and crossed the street against a "Do Not Walk" light. The last of the chasers quit as they watched Larry walking to the garage.

"Not used to reporters yet, huh?" said a tall, white-yellow-haired old man waiting for Larry. The old man wore a worn-out gray pair of pants and a wrinkled white business shirt with the sleeves rolled up. He held no recorder.

"No."

*"Don't talk to him,"* Lar ordered.

"What are you going to do?" asked the old man as he slowly started walking with Larry.

"About what?"

*"I told you not to talk to him."*

Larry took a deep breath to retake control and slowed his walk to the old man's pace in rebellion. This one old straggler was all that was left.

"Marilyn Ramirez—Simms's going to get her," the old guy said calmly, enjoying that he'd guessed how the press trap would work, and now he had the lawyer to himself. "When are you going to make a deal?"

Larry shook his head and kept walking.

"Off the record," the old man said. "I'm Doug Lacy, columnist at the *Chronicle*." They shook hands as they continued walking in the shade to the garage.

"I know who you are." Lacy wrote about Brian a few times, the last time questioning the police conclusion of suicide. Larry thought then he had an ally who would fight for the truth, but Lacy never wrote another column about it, unless Larry had missed it while he was in the hospital. He couldn't be too hard on Lacy anyway since Larry let Brian down, too.

"Off the record?" Larry asked.

"Off the record. I'm looking for *background*." Lacy emphasized the last word.

"Off the record," Larry repeated, nervous because of his inexperience with reporters and the potential for misunderstandings, "I don't know yet. Stonek just got shot yesterday, and I don't know much yet."

They reached the multistory garage, and Lacy grabbed his arm and said in his gravelly smoker voice, "What are you doing on this case anyway? You don't belong on it. You never had a serious criminal case until Bain, and you never figured out what that was all about. Did you know Ramirez before she was arrested?"

Larry didn't need any truth or insightful questions, and he didn't need to tell this old fox, even off the record, what was going on, as if he even knew the answers. "No, didn't know her. I guess I was hired because I'm so famous." Larry broke free and stepped through the heavy garage door.

Larry drove out of the garage on the phone answering Miller's angry questions about what happened and what he told the press.

"You should have gone through the tunnel the way I told you," Miller said.

David called and said Simms and the DA had called. Larry told him to have the office call them back and tell them he was meeting with his client today. They'd confirm that when they watched the local news.

"You OK?" David asked.

"Yeah, I just got trapped by a bunch of reporters because of my own stupidity."

Larry intended to drive back to his hotel, but he turned home instead. He didn't know what had happened in the room with Marilyn, but he needed to see his wife. She was always there for him; they'd always had a great love life since high school. Diane stayed thin and sleek, and their lovemaking was a constant even when his madness drove her away or drove her to throw him out for Katie's and Danny's safety. Even now, she was still there for him when he needed her.

"Hey," he said when she answered her cell.

"Hey." Diane was surprised.

"Can I come over?"

Quiet, she knew why he called. She could read his mind by the sound of his voice when he was normal.

"Well, I had…what's wrong?" She sounded worried.

"I need you, honey." He loved saying "honey" again like he used to, and he couldn't resist.

"Sure; come on. How long before you get here?"

"Twenty minutes."

Larry drove up the long driveway past freshly cut grass and newly planted yellow and red flowers, up behind his former two-story home. He walked through the back kitchen door and saw Carmen. She was the maid/babysitter/cook, who'd worked for them and now Diane. She was bent over stacking plates in the dishwasher with her back to him. "Carmen," he shouted.

"Aiy, madre de dios," Carmen screamed as she jumped and turned to face him, and then she smiled, laughed at herself, and said, "Mr. Larry, you scared me."

"How are you?" Larry walked in and inhaled his former home. He smelled bacon Carmen cooked for Danny's and Katie's breakfast and all the other smells of a clean and happy home.

"Good." She drew it out with a genuine smile. Fifty, a Colombian immigrant, she worked all day here before going home and working until late for her own family. Still smiling and happy to see him, she took a bottled water from the refrigerator and handed it to Larry. "Miss Diane say you're coming. She upstairs." Larry took the cold bottle with a thank you and ran up the back stairs two at a time and knocked on his own old bedroom door.

"Larry?" Diane called.

"Yes, can I come in?"

"Yes."

Larry stepped in and locked the door behind him. The bedroom was unchanged. A king-size bed with an oak headboard sat at the far end of the large room, which was just as he remembered it—spotlessly clean, with flowery curtains and comforter splashing color across the room. A sixty-inch wall television hung high to his left was set to the music-only cable jazz station. As he walked in, he could hear the familiar sounds Diane made through the slightly open bathroom door when she set things down on the counter: there was the perfume bottle, the next sound was the lotion…it was effortless poetry.

"I'll be right out. What happened, Larry?"

He sat on the edge of the bed. Diane had left his chests of drawers and pictures of the family with him in them in the room. "How'd you know?"

Diane stepped out of the bathroom, and they looked deep into each other's eyes, knowing and wanting each other. His eyes drifted to her white, smooth skin and almost white, blond hair. She was naked, and as she stepped to him, he was overwhelmed that she went to all this effort. She was still there when he needed her.

She sat next to him, really on him, and kissed him like she still loved him. He wrapped his arms gently around her and lightly pulled her onto his lap. He smelled the special perfume she always wore when they planned to make love.

She softly pulled away from the kiss even as he held her closer, as close as if the bad had never happened. She whispered, "What happened?" She looked worried and moved her eyebrows. "It's that new case you're on. You shouldn't take on something like that; you know you can't take that kind of pressure."

It might have sounded like nagging or griping to someone else, but from their long, loving marriage, Larry felt in his whole being that it was love and caring, and he loved her for it. "It's more. It's different. It's not the case."

Diane hid her worried eyebrows, kissed his ear and then his hair, and they slowly rolled onto the bed.

After they finished, Diane kissed him and slipped into the shower.

On his way back to his downtown hotel, he checked his cell, and it was full of calls—minions, David, Simms, and Brian's mother.

# CHAPTER 12

"**O**h, thank God, thank you so much for calling." She sucked air. "The police called. A nice man came by—kind of odd—said he was checking on Brian's death. I was so grateful I thought everyone but us just forgot him."

"Slow down, Mrs. Bain."

"I'm so sorry, Mr. Lamb It's just I've been so sad, so depressed, you know. No one cared what happened to my poor boy; they just wanted him to disappear. I've been so sad."

"Mrs. Bain…" When she wouldn't stop talking, he yelled, "Mrs. Bain." She'd go on like this for a long time if he didn't interrupt her.

"I'm sorry, so sorry, Mr. Lamb. I'm just, you know, so relieved. Thank you, Jesus. That nice Detective Simms said you were helping him; thank you so much. Thank God. We're the only ones that haven't forgotten my sweet boy. I love him so much my heart hurts so much; it's all I ever think about."

"What happened when Detective Simms came to visit you?" Larry spoke loudly and clearly so she'd stop and listen.

"Just as I said, you know, the police called; well, Detective Simms called. Asked if he could come by. Scared me to death, God bless his soul. He was right out here asking me all about Brian."

Larry called her first on his cell as he drove down the highway in the fresh dark to his hotel. He'd always call Mrs. Bain first—the hardworking, very poor, and heartbroken old woman who gave Larry her life savings of $2,500 to defend her son, brought Larry homemade cookies, kissed his head, and thanked God for bringing him into their lives every time she brought her son to an attorney-client meeting. Larry didn't know this type of person still existed before he met her outside the Waller County Courthouse.

"Anyway, you know he came to see me. Detective Simms, silly-looking man, really tall; he's so tall, moves funny, like he's all broken up and didn't heal right, you know? God bless him, but he said he, you know, was checking the facts on Brian's death; God bless him for that. He asked who Brian was afraid of. Poor boy, I miss him so much, and the nice detective asked where Brian was the last two days and who he talked to."

"Good, good," Larry yelled. "I hoped he'd check into it. He told me he would, but we've heard that before."

"I know, I know, it's terrible how they let my poor boy—I love him so much—let his murderer just get away."

"What else did Detective Simms ask?"

"Well, just all that you know stuff, the facts stuff; he was so kind. A real gentleman, he promised to try all he could. I know he will, you know, try as hard as he can."

"I'll call him tomorrow and thank him, Mrs. Bain, and see what we can do to help him." Larry liked that Simms moved so fast to check on Brian's murder, and it was a nice distraction from Marilyn's investigation. Maybe Larry could have a couple of days without any new crisis so he'd have time to figure out what he was going to do about her case.

"Oh, God bless you, I know you will, Mr. Larry. Thank you so much. I told the nice, you know, detective you would; you've been so kind; you always were to my poor boy. I miss him so much. I'm all alone now; it's so terrible. He only trusted you. You saved his life getting him out of that terrible jail. I just wish you'd been able to see him, you know. He said you talked to him and were going to see him that last day."

"What, Mrs. Bain?" He guessed she was still confused; she was always confused about days, and explaining that he'd never talked to Brian that day or that she had her days or memory wrong about the murder of her son would have been cruel. She'd never get it straight anyway. "I'll call Detective Simms tomorrow. You try to get some rest."

"All right; God bless you…"

Larry had his cheeseburger and bourbon at the far end of the hotel bar lined up next to that of all the other, deservedly or not, divorced men. Most of them saw one another almost every night, gathering like crows on an electric line at dusk, to sit on the same stool in the same bar and talk about the same subjects, while their ex-wives and children ate in homes the men paid for, doing the family things these men didn't get to do anymore.

After Mrs. Bain, Larry didn't check any more voice mails; he just didn't have the stomach for it. He just wanted to escape his world, dwell on making love to Diane, and wonder what Danny and Katie were doing at that moment. He drifted into that world as he ate, while he still heard the familiar babble around him about who was going to win some football game, who was playing or hurt, or who had to pay the most child support and why it was unfair. The paradox was that this pathetic state was the happiest Larry had been in a year.

He woke late the next morning, and before he could get a shirt on, his office called. "The police said they'd be here in two hours."

"Who called?" Larry asked. He knew it wasn't the police, just Simms, and he hated the way his office, small and practicing simple law, reacted like a drama queen on just a phone call. It was inconvenient. Larry skipped his run and headed straight to the office. Detective Simms stomped into Larry's office thirty minutes after he got there.

Larry told the assistant to pull the Bain file from closed files, but she was busy drinking coffee and talking on the phone, Larry still hadn't reviewed the file by the time Simms arrived. Detective Simms came into Larry's office with his own fresh cup that the panicky receptionist poured for him as he explained a better way to grind coffee to improve flavor. As he entered Larry's office, he made several comments about the wasted square footage of the office and how the halls were too wide, and Larry began to get a headache.

"Thank you for helping me." Simms shook Larry's hand and sat down. Simms's monologues wandered from observing the type of computer Larry's office used and what type would have been better to how nice and sunny the weather was. Simms wore another dark suit—he apparently liked them—but Larry noticed his pants legs were cut high, like Simms expected to walk through a flood. More likely they were cut high to show off his expensive black cowboy boots. His crooked mustache that morning looked like it had been taped under his nose.

"Mrs. Bain told me you called her."

"What a nice, nice old lady she is. She's so brokenhearted." Simms slid up to the edge of his chair, studying Larry. "I think she'd given up."

"Thank you for being so nice to her." Larry leaned back. He didn't like Simms closing the space between them, even a few inches.

"Of course, of course. Boy, she sure believes in you. She thinks you were always her son's savior." Simms sat back in his chair, sipped his coffee, and watched.

"I doubt that." Larry began to admit the truth, but realized that he couldn't reveal his true legal limitations to Simms, even as a joke, so instead he said, "I just mean that his mom was always helping Brian, no matter what he did."

Simms stood up and paced around the office, checking pictures on the wall of Larry, Diane, and the kids. He pulled out and flipped through several books from the shelves. He'd now looked at more lawbooks on Larry's shelves than Larry ever had.

"I know she has, and you hadn't had much criminal experience before you were on Bain's case either."

"True," Larry said, shocked Simms knew that. It was obvious Simms had looked Larry up—and what had he found? An inexperienced lazy attorney who was in a mental hospital six months ago. That must have terrified him.

Simms stopped and looked at Larry. "Are you gonna let me talk to Miss Ramirez?"

"Nope; you've got to give something. What are you going to give me?"

Simms laughed. "I'm not gonna give you anything. I'm gonna execute her if I can."

"I don't think so. Stonek bonded out in, what, thirty minutes?"

"Yeah." Simms drew it out, disgusted.

"I think you're looking a little weak, my friend. I know what you have." Thanks to Legs and Miller. Larry wondered where they'd been. Right after Don Stonek was arrested, Larry's phone battery ran down from their calls, but since Stonek bonded out, Larry hadn't heard anything from them. "And you don't have anything: two shooters with no idea who they talked to, nothing from my client, and I'll put money you got shit from Stonek."

"I need another coffee. You're killing me, Lamb." Simms walked out, and Larry toasted himself with his cup, and then he opened his Bain file to quickly check whether there was anything that he didn't want Simms to see.

When Simms loped back, he complained, "Nobody's talkin', I'll admit it, but I know they did it, planned it together, and I'll figure it out."

"You think you can figure just about anything out, don't you?" Larry slid his Bain file across to Simms.

"I think so, if I have enough time." Simms opened the file.

"I hope so, at least for Brian. That's my file. I didn't see anything in it that'll help you, but I hope I'm wrong."

"Can I take it?"

"Hell, no."

"Have a spare office?"

"Two doors down, but the file's not thick enough to take you long."

"I have my methods," he said as he left. "Thanks."

# CHAPTER 13

"**I** want to talk to him," Marilyn said. She no longer sat across the table, but as soon as she walked into the box, she scraped a chair around the corner and put it next to him. As she sat, Larry saw the angry bearded guard staring at her through the cross wired, bulletproof-glass door window, but he didn't come in to make her move. He just glared, and when she didn't bother to notice him, his face faded away.

Before she came in, Larry was sick of Marilyn: Sick of the reporters, sick of Simms, sick of the constant twenty-four-hour obsession of her and her problems. He had no space for his own life. He couldn't see his kids or even check his investments. It was always Marilyn, her needs, her latest catastrophe. Either the police called about her or Bain, or Legs called with a new brief, or she used to, or his office called in a panic. When he was left alone, he worried about it like acid slowly burning through his insides, burning until nothing would be left of Larry but a nasty, crusty hole. And Lar ate away at him, too. He was the real acid, and he was winning. Larry felt him all the time now—inside, stirring, controlling, restless.

Marilyn sat close enough for him to imagine the scent of withering roses over the slight smell of vomit from the room, and he had to think to breathe. She was different now. She touched him, not just physically, but intimately—the way her foot accidentally touched his and how her hips moved. She began to act like they were lovers, but that was impossible because as long as they had known each other, she'd been in jail; in fact, he'd never seen her outside this box.

"Larry?"

"Yeah." He came out of his fantasy and back into the cell.

"I want to talk to Simms."

"No."

"I want to."

"Nothing good can come of it."

"Larry," she said in her wanting and promising tone, and he loved it when she used it, even knowing it was to pry something out of him.

"What?" he said.

"I want to," she said pouty—not demanding.

"Marilyn." When he first interviewed her, he'd asked her if she'd hired the killers. He'd believed her, at least during their visits, but he couldn't let her talk to Simms. Legs and Miller insisted he never ask her whether she'd actually done it, but what did twelve-year-olds know? "You'll screw it up." Larry said. She'd already admitted to Simms when he first arrested her that she knew the two men arrested for attempted murder, and Larry suspected she'd know the third man as soon as the police found him.

"I know him," she said.

"Who?"

"Simms—he's questioned me, and I know him."

"Oh."

"And you don't have to worry. I've known his type lots of times. I can handle him."

"Can't do it."

"Why?"

"Because you can get in trouble. It's like a cop pulls you over in a car and asks you if you had a drink. If you say a couple, even if it's true, they immediately interpret it as an admission that you're drunk and driving, and they arrest you. You can't control intentional misinterpretations of what you say and how they might represent it to the court, so, no, you can't talk."

Her foot touched his leg. "Then you'll have to do it for me. That way you can control the words."

*"We'll do it."* Larry felt the pressure, and it let Lar out. Marilyn smiled like she heard it and recognized him, but she couldn't—he only spoke in Larry's head.

"I knew you would," she said.

"Would what?" Larry said.

"Talk to Simms for me," she said.

*"Of course we will."*

"I didn't say I would," Larry said.

"You just did," she said.

"No, I didn't," Larry said.

*"Yes, we did; I'm sorry."*

Marilyn's lips curled slightly as she lowered her gaze to meet his. "Larry..." she said in a breathless whisper that was pure desire.

He was lost in her incredible blue eyes, not remembering anything but how he felt about her at that moment.

"Sometimes...another side of you comes out...sometimes...doesn't it, Larry?"

"No." How did she know?

*"You're bright; only three others have really even known about me."*

"I know," Marilyn said.

Was he talking out loud? He was talking out loud. How was she responding to what Larry heard in his head otherwise?

"You know what?" Larry asked.

She looked at him. The harsh conditions in jail hadn't affected her silky soft skin, full lips, and dark lashes framing those amazing eyes.

"I know, Larry...your other side," she said.

"There's no other side."

*"She knows, dumbass."*

Larry tried to slam the door in his head, over and over, but the latch wouldn't click anymore.

*"It won't work anymore; I'm out."*

"Don't worry, Larry, I'm not going to tell anyone. It's still your secret," she said.

Larry couldn't talk. How did this happen? How did this woman, a prisoner, my client, find this out? "It's not true, Marilyn."

"Larry, you talk to me as the other guy; of course it's true." She smiled, and then the smile turned to laughter. "Don't worry; both of you can talk to Simms."

*"What do we want?"*

"Where is he? What's Simms know? I need to know what he has on Don. That fucker got arrested and back out in about thirty minutes. Simms won't get anything from him," she said.

"I don't know. I can talk to Simms about that, but he's going to want to know what you know about it, and you already told me you don't know anything about the attacks."

*"Dude,"* Lar said in disbelief at Larry's assumptions. Then to her, Lar said, *"We'll see where his head's at."*

"Good," she said.

"What?" Larry asked.

As Lar walked out of the jail, he called the detective. "Simms." Larry heard the answer to his phone, shocked, but he was only a spectator.

*"Detective? We need to talk,"* Lar said.

"Yes, we do."

*"Now?"*

"Yeah, can you come over to my office?"

Police Headquarters was just across downtown. *"Sure; I can be there in fifteen minutes."*

"Good. I'll let 'em know downstairs at the front desk to expect you."

When they got there, an officer was waiting and walked them to Simms's office.

"Fifteen, on the button," Simms said. He was wearing his testify-in-court suit, but his jacket hung on a hanger on the doorknob and his sleeves were rolled up. "What were you visiting—the jail?"

*"Actually, I was."*

"Good; you gonna let me bring her over?"

*"Not today."*

"She's in trouble; I've got two men ready to say anything, Stonek's not going to help her."

*"You have nothing, and you're going to let Stonek go. You. Don't. Have. Shit. And I'm not worried about DA Johnson."*

Simms knew Chris Johnson never got a conviction on Bain—the scandal interfered; in any case, that was irrelevant to what Simms wanted to accomplish right then, so he ignored it.

*"You have two guys who don't know who the fuck they talked to. That's it, and that's all you'll ever have."*

"I may have another soon, and the game may change," Simms said, trying to bluff this suddenly completely different attorney. "If you're going to make a deal with me, you need to do it before I don't need your lady anymore."

Chris Johnson walked in. "Hey, Larry."

*"Oh, I'm ganged up on,"* Lar said as he stood and shook hands.

"I can see how worried you are," replied the DA.

"I thought Chris might help us talk about coming to some kind of agreement," Simms said.

"I didn't come over prepared to talk about a deal today," Larry butted in.

*"But what do you have in mind?"* Lar added.

Chris sat down and dug through his large western leather briefcase styled like a small saddle while Simms sat back in his chair across the desk studying Larry.

"We want her to testify against Stonek," Chris mumbled as he dug.

"We can give her ten years if she does," Simms said.

*"Shh, ten, that's bull."* Lar drew out the last word. *"I want her dismissed."*

Chris looked up and said with no sign of any emotion in his voice or on his face, "You know that's not going to happen."

"I'm not saying we're going to do anything," Larry inserted. He was frustrated that Lar kept talking, and worse, that the DA and Simms could hear him and were listening to him.

"I know what you're saying…" Simms stared intently at Larry.

"But if you do say something, don't say dismiss," Chris joked, but his face still showed no emotion—only sarcasm. "Sit back down."

Larry—not realizing he was standing, sat.

"She already all but told me she knows what's going on, Larry. She's just too careful with her words. Get her to give Stonek up, and she'll be out in half the time," Simms said.

*"I can't go talk to her with ten. She doesn't even know we're here; she'd be pissed if she knew it,"* Lar said.

Simms noticed the "we" and noted to himself that it wasn't the first reference.

"Look, we have a good history together," Chris said. "You're an honest guy; I respect you. You know I'm not going to dismiss; I can give you seven, maybe five." Chris didn't move as he spoke; he just sat there with his oversize light brown briefcase with papers hanging out of it sitting in his lap, watching Larry, not for any particular reason—just that he visually wanted to communicate nothing.

Lar noticed and decided to do the opposite. He twitched and shook his head, scratched his arm, stood up, sat down quickly, and said, *"Five years, five years? No, no."* Larry watched how Lar acted, unprofessional and erratic, but he couldn't stop him.

Simms leaned up, picked up something to tap against the desk, took a drink of coffee, and said, "Larry...Larry, calm down. We'll work this out. I can see we're coming to something—just relax."

*"Can't go with five, though,"* Lar said. Larry made him sit back down and appear to relax, but then Lar said, *"Not five—one."*

Chris looked at him like Larry had finally said something worth paying attention to.

Larry thought this was bad because now he was negotiating time, but Lar knew it meant he might get one, maybe dismiss. Larry's phone rang—Legs. He hadn't heard from her for a while, and she probably somehow knew where he was right now. Lar turned the phone off. He didn't need any more instructions from her; he knew if Larry was too stupid to figure out that they worked for Stonek, he wasn't. They could fuck themselves, if he didn't do it to them first.

"Can't do one. She tried to kill a woman three times," Chris said, raising his voice as he spoke.

Lar knew Chris didn't really care; he was just negotiating. *"No, you get Stonek; you don't give a shit about the nobodies. You should dismiss her."*

"You said one," Simms yelled.

"What the hell is Lar doing? What the hell am I saying?" thought Larry. "Dismiss, one year, dismiss, jumping around—they're going to think I'm crazy."

*"That's before I thought about how little you really care about her. You don't care; no one does. Just let her go afterward,"* Lar said.

"Can't do that," Chris said.

*"You can do anything you want. It's why you came over here. You're famous,"* Lar said.

"Famous 'cause of you," Chris said in his dry cowboy tone.

*"Not me."*

"Lamb?" Simms said.

"Yeah," Chris said, thinking about Lar's comment.

"I visited Mrs. Bain," Simms said.

Larry said, "I know that." He could feel Lar back out and allow Larry to breathe.

"Two years. That's the best I can do," Chris conceded. "But she's got to testify Stonek was the…involved in the murder attempts and knew they meant to kill his wife."

"She said you were very nice to her. Thank you," Larry said to Simms.

"She's a nice lady. Been through a lot of terrible heartache."

"Can we get back on Ramirez?" Chris said.

"Yeah, I'll talk to her about it," Larry said to Chris. "I'll talk to her."

"Good," Chris said, shoving papers into his case and snapping it shut as he stood up. He shook hands with Simms and Larry as he said, "Call me after you talk, and don't mess around." And then he was gone.

Simms sat back down and said, "Sit down."

"What's left?" Larry said.

"I want to tell you about what I found out from Mrs. Bain. Maybe you can help me."

Larry sat on the edge of his seat.

"Coffee?" Simms asked as he finished his old, cold cup.

"No. How can you drink that stuff?"

"It's so bad in the first place that it's hard to tell the difference."

"Then you should stop on the way to the office and get something better."

"Who goes home? It's just that Mrs. Bain talked to Brian the day he died," Simms said as he worked toward his test. He pretended to concentrate on what some papers said in front of him as he spoke, but what he really did was pay close attention to how Lamb reacted.

"I know that. Hell, I may have been the one that told the police that way back when they actually acted like they were going to investigate it," Larry said.

"She happened to say that you'd talked to Brian that morning, too."

"Really? I don't remember that," Larry said. "I don't remember her saying anything about that before." He could feel Lar drift farther away, liberating Larry's mind.

"She said"—Simms pushed his chair back, crossed his legs, and wiped something off his polished black cowboy boots as he watched—"that he was waiting on you, that you'd called and said you were on your way to meet him."

Larry was completely puzzled by this. It was impossible that she'd told Simms that because it never happened. "That's not right." Larry wondered why Simms would lie about this. He didn't think he'd called Brian that morning, and he knew he didn't tell Brian he was driving to meet him.

"She never told the police that—not that they asked many questions. They were in such a hurry to just close their file." Larry was searching his memory, looking for why Mrs. Bain might tell Simms this. When he couldn't find a reason, he concluded Simms must be lying about it to get some reaction from him, but why would he do that?

"I'm just wondering—did you drive up to meet Brian that day?"

"No, of course not. If I'd done that, I'd have told someone," Larry said, his stomach hollow from the ache caused by Simms's question. Everyone abandoned Brian, everyone but him, and when he finally gets someone to look into Brian's murder, he gets this type of surreal question.

"Larry?"

"Yeah."

"You checked yourself into the hospital right after that, didn't you?"

"What's that got to do with anything?"

Simms looked at him blankly. "Nothing; just thought that's why you might not remember it."

"It's not; it's because I didn't. I'd remember that. I couldn't even get the police to investigate it when I found out; they'd already cleaned the scene up."

"What were you doing that day?"

"I was on my computer and at the law library all day trying to figure out how I was going to get Brian into Witness Protection."

"Which library—the county law library?"

"No, I just had some books and downloaded stuff; no one goes to the library anymore, do they?"

"Do you still have those books?"

"What are you doing? Why are you asking me this?"

"Because I have to. Once Mrs. Bain said you might have seen Bain the day he died, I have to check on you. Thorough, you know," Simms said, apologizing.

"I still don't know why she'd say that. Are you sure she said it? Did you get her confused? She may have been confused. She's a simple woman; she's been so sad for so long. If you asked her a lot of questions, she could get really confused."

Simms just allowed Lamb to talk, but he wasn't really saying anything. Once Lamb relaxed, Simms said, "I don't know; it could have been anything. I don't know why she said it; she just said it, so now I have to ask you about it."

Larry breathed now. He felt better, and he could feel Lar nowhere around him, and he said, "I understand that; I want you to. I've fought to get somebody to do what you're doing, and I'm grateful you're doing it, so if I have to answer a couple of questions because poor Mrs. Bain muttered something, I'm good with it."

"Thanks."

"So, what was your question? No, I don't know where those books went. I don't remember what happened to them after I went to the hospital."

"Where'd you go?"

"Saint Louis Medical Center."

"I'm afraid, Mr. Lamb, I'm going to have to check with your doctor. I'm sorry, but because of what Mrs. Bain said, I must be thorough, I'll be brief; I won't invade."

"I understand. I hate it, of course, that you have to, but you do." Larry took an old business card from his wallet and held it out to Simms. "My doctor is Henderson. I don't know why I still have his card; I don't need it anymore. You take it. If you need me to call and let him know you're going to contact him, I'll be glad to—if it'll get you on in your investigation."

"Slow down; you're talking a hundred miles an hour." But Simms took the card and said, "Thanks. It'll let me get on with it and on to the important characters."

"If we're done"—Larry stood—"I guess I need to go talk to my client."

"It's pretty late; you'll probably have to wait until tomorrow." Simms needed some time before he saw Lamb again.

"Fine. I'll talk to her in the morning and come by."

"I think I have to appear in court tomorrow; I'll call you when I get out." That way he could ensure he had enough time to call Mrs. Bain again and go by Saint Louis.

# CHAPTER 14

"It's impossible. I won't talk to you," Dr. Henderson shouted at Detective Simms. They sat in Henderson's office. It was a dark room, dark walls and bookshelves, the opposite of what Simms expected a psychiatrist's office would look like. It was more a corporate president's study. Dr. Henderson was about sixty-five, fat, white-haired, and pale.

"You've Mr. Lamb's permission to talk with me." Simms wasn't asking.

"That's correct, but I don't believe he understands that."

"Of course not; he's not a doctor. He doesn't properly appreciate the nature of what you do," Simms thought to himself. Simms constantly had to wade through doctors' egos to get what he needed. He expected this reaction; he'd have been disappointed if he hadn't gotten it, but he didn't expect the ferocity with which Henderson said no.

"Doctor, I just have a couple of questions to clear up some details. It won't take long; I'm sure you'll consider them trivial."

"His treatment was never completed; it would not be in his best interest to discuss it."

"I'm not investigating Mr. Lamb. We have information that requires me to check on parts of Mr. Lamb's location after last July 28."

The doctor said nothing, but flipped from page to page of the file reading and buying time as he reconsidered. Simms let the stew simmer.

"He was here," Henderson said as he raised his chin. His stomach rolled with each breath, and his chest popped every couple of minutes to get more air. He turned some pages of the precious file he refused to let Simms see.

"You said he wasn't through with his treatment?"

"Of course not. What Mr.…." Henderson stopped himself. "He checked himself out against our advice."

Simms crossed his legs and looked at his boot. As he tried to wipe the side of his boot with his hand, he asked, "What was Mr. Lamb's diagnosis?"

"See, that's the point—I do not believe I should discuss it. There can be evolving diagnoses over the course of therapy, and laymen misinterpret the connotations."

"The doctor could balance a coffee cup on his belly if he tried," Simms thought.

"Depression?" Simms asked.

"What? He gave me permission, I know…"

"I see the signed form on the top of the file in front of you," Simms said.

"I still cannot share details."

"Just an overview for a layman."

"To put in terms you can understand, I initially diagnosed the patient with severe symptoms of bipolar, anxiety, and dissociative personality disorder, as well as an addiction to prescription diet pills."

"Dissociative…"

"Dual personality; that part of the diagnosis was quite controversial with my colleagues, and after…" Dr. Henderson put his half reading glasses on and squinted as he read the file. He lifted several pages closer, but he spoke as if he remembered it all clearly without reading. "However, after the first three sessions, I was quite confident of my diagnosis. I prescribed the proper medication for my findings as a whole, but only to be initiated after his prescription drug addiction detox."

"I'm amazed at how well you remember the details of past patients." Simms led the doctor.

"I confess I usually don't, but Mr. Lamb was exceptional from the beginning. His dissociative personality disorder revealed itself in a separate identity that Mr. Lamb appeared unaware of. However, after approximately two more sessions, the symptoms abruptly disappeared. This was incongruous for this disorder, and my colleagues believed that I may have misdiagnosed symptoms from his other psychoses."

Simms was satisfied; the doctor told him far more than he had to—or than Simms had asked for.

"His other symptoms appreciatively improved over the next month until the patient terminated his in-house treatment. After he left Saint Louis, he did attend two outpatient counseling sessions, and then he terminated the counseling sessions as well."

"Did you consider refusing to allow him to leave?"

The doctor wrinkled his face at the question, and said, "No. There was no basis—no legal basis—in fact, no medical basis to consider that. His objective symptoms had, as I said, appreciatively improved—stabilized actually. There was no sign of the subjective symptoms that created the challenged initial diagnosis of dissociative disorder. He was no danger to himself or anyone else. So absolutely not."

Simms showed nothing—his poker face was clear. "Could he have hidden his symptoms of double personality?"

"Dissociative personality disorder?"

"Uh, yes...that...from you?"

"I don't believe it's possible to intentionally conceal it from me. He initially couldn't remember certain times and behaviors during a critical stage."

"And then it disappeared?"

"Yes. This would be extremely unlikely for this diagnosis and stimulated a reevaluation of the conclusions. He couldn't fool me."

Simms didn't listen to the last part of the answer. "Could he have unintentionally concealed it from you? Could his other personality have hidden from you?"

The doctor looked surprised as he sipped his drink. He looked Simms in the eye and banged the glass onto his desk. "Have you researched this?"

"Yes, some. A little."

"I'm aware of a study that indicates an example of that, and it was highly subjective. I certainly don't believe Mr. Lamb was doing that."

"But you don't believe he suddenly quit suffering from it either?"

"No." Henderson growled and scratched as he tried to take a breath and clear his throat. "I don't; that's why I may have given more weight to some of his symptoms during my preliminary examinations."

That's all Simms was going to get out of this doctor. Simms doubted he'd get more even with a warrant, and he'd never get one on Lamb. "Thank you, Doctor."

"Are we done?"

"I told you it would be short."

Larry entered the new twenty-one-story criminal courthouse through the antiseptic underground tunnel between the fifteen-story car garages and the courthouses. Underneath, the tunnel was quiet, clean, and air-conditioned. The masses—the overflowing crowd of men and women with criminal charges against them, their scared spouses, screaming children, bewildered friends, and other frightened family—were on the ground floor struggling to get through creeping, antiquated security machines and unmotivated guards.

Too few elevators waited for them on the other side. By now, they were all panicked about getting to their courtrooms on time because this was Houston. And Houston judges freely revoked bail and threw the unconvicted back in jail. Defendants all feared it, but Larry, with other attorneys and jail and courthouse personnel, knew about the tunnel. Few told the unwashed masses.

Down here, the machines worked, and the guards greeted you with a smile and a good morning, so everyone slid through security and right up the elevator. When Larry's elevator door opened on the nineteenth floor, the noise of the crowd burst in, and the cameramen with their giant, black television cameras charged at him. Young reporters with perfect hair rushed, shouting questions. A camera light clicked on and lit the hallway like an exploding star, and Larry could see nothing as he stepped into the hall. Between the reporters and their cameramen stood the puzzled criminal defendants and their families waiting for their own court settings, ignorant of the chaos that engulfed them. The judge sent deputies and bailiffs out to quiet the roar. Larry couldn't work through the crowd to get to his courtroom; he couldn't see where it was, and he couldn't hear any of the questions shouted at him.

Someone grabbed his arm and squeezed it hard. Larry's eyes adjusted to the lights, and he saw Legs gripping his arm. Her piercing eyes shot through any haze in his mind, and he understood without her saying a word that this was serious and followed her as she bulldozed through the people and toward the 269th District courtroom's outer doors. Bailiffs barred reporters from following, and the two stood in the sound lock, where defendants talked to attorneys, wrapped up phone calls, and tucked in their shirttails before entering.

Legs looked in both side conference rooms, but they were full, and then she shoved her face in his. "Why haven't you been returning your calls?"

"I haven't gotten any calls. Am I dealing with you or Miller?"

"They're going to try to get you to make a deal; we're not going to interfere in your negotiations."

Her haircut squared her face, and in fact, if it weren't for the severe cut of that and her dark business suit, which made her look indistinguishable from other female lawyers, she could have looked OK. As he walked through the inner courtroom doors, he looked back at Legs. "Good; I didn't ask you to."

Larry entered a new, different frenetic world now. He stood next to the jury box to orientate himself.

"What are you going to ask the DA for?" whispered one attorney to another as they stopped next to him. The air rushed through the vent in the ceiling above him.

"I..." the other began to answer, but stopped as the bailiff stomped by giving him a foul look.

Then, turning to the defendants sitting in the audience, the bailiff demanded, "Go outside, you sir, out. All shirttails tucked in, even T-shirts." He escorted the frightened man out the door and then slowly walked through the audience to spot any other rule violation.

"I think three years; he has two priors." The attorney finished his answer now that the bailiff was busy.

"Haven't you talked to her about it yet?" Legs angrily whispered behind Larry, and then he walked into the side conference room that held the female prisoners. Larry sat on a steel stool and looked through the two-inch clear plastic. He spoke through tiny holes drilled into it to the women prisoners in a cement cell: "Marilyn Ramirez." A guard listened nearby, but pretended not to. Marilyn came up and put her ear on the plastic holes so she could hear him.

"You talk to the detective, Larry?" she yelled, but Larry barely heard her.

"Yeah; he's down to eighteen months, but I don't think we should do it."

"I want it dismissed. If he'll dismiss it, I'll give him what he wants."

That surprised Larry. Marilyn always said she wasn't involved in the shootings, just knew the first two men. That was ridiculous, of course, but that's what she said. Larry knew she dated Stonek before she was arrested. That was all over the news every night and on the top of the newspaper's web page.

His brain clicked, and he felt it. *"I'll take care of it. We've just got to keep Simms busy catching Stonek,"* Lar said to Marilyn. Then he said to Larry, *"That's all he needs to do."* He's back, thought Larry, and what did he mean when he said to Larry that Simms needed to stay busy only trying to convict Stonek?

"I know you will. That's what I want him busy doing. Will you"—she looked at the guard and tried to say in a way that he couldn't overhear— "be available when I get out of here?"

*"Of course I will."* Lar smiled. *"We'll just reset this hearing two weeks. It may be done by then."*

"Good. Will I hear from you today?"

*"I don't know. Simms was supposed to meet us today, but he put us off with an excuse, so we'll have to see what he's up to."*

"OK," she said as she stood up and drifted back into the mass of waiting prisoners.

"What are we going to do?" asked Chris. The assistant DA stood next to Lar in the courtroom, with the judge on the bench waiting for a hearing to start, aggravated at the chaos on his floor and that he'd be part of the main story on the news that night and in front of a broad table with stacks of files of the hundred criminal defendants that had their hearings set that morning. Other attorneys walked back and forth between talking to the three DAs assigned to the court, the packed audience of frightened defendants, and the court clerks at their desks along one wall, busily resetting cases, handing out papers, and revoking bail on defendants who showed up late. Chris was just assigned to the Ramirez case, or rather, now that their target for conviction was Stonek, the Stonek case.

It's never a good thing when a DA's office assigns a special prosecutor to your client's case—even Larry knew that. If the DA was so interested in your client that they assigned a special prosecutor plus resources just to get her convicted, they'd usually bury her. "Lar's right; we'll have to deal," Larry thought.

*"My client's going to solve your problems, and you're going to dismiss her charges,"* Lar whispered.

"No," Chris said, exhibiting a believable face of disagreement, but Lar knew Chris was weak. "We'll reset this."

*"You heard from Simms yet?"*

"No, I'm waiting for him to call. He said he had something this morning. He finds that third guy before you make a deal, she'll be toast." Johnson was trying to cut off negotiations.

*"I don't think so. Besides, you haven't even caught anyone yet,"* Lar said. *"And if you do, they probably won't know any more than the last two dumbasses."*

"You seem pretty confident in your lady."

*"Just a logical conclusion from the other two. People don't change."*

"You have. When we were dealing with just a little misdemeanor six months ago, you weren't this confident about anything."

*"I was a dumbass, too."*

Lar reset the case and went to tell Marilyn, but she'd already been returned to the jail, and then he stepped into the halls to brave the excited horde.

Lar pushed out of the courtroom doors into the waiting hysteria, the crowd so compressed that the reporters in front couldn't move back to give him a step of space. He could only see the first few layers of excited faces, but he stopped for a moment to let the wave of knowledge that he was there roll back to the rest of the crowd. When the screaming pitch doubled, he pretended to try to step through the crowd to the elevator.

"What happened in the hearing?"

"Did you reset?"

"When's it set for?"

"Did you talk to the DA?"

"Are you going to make a deal?"

"What's…"

Lar announced, *"They have no evidence against Miss Ramirez. It's an outrage that the judge refuses to even set bail and allow her to leave jail. The district attorney and police are holding an innocent woman in jail in an attempt to force her to admit to something she was not involved in, and I can guarantee you it won't work."* "That's pretty good; that sounds pretty good," Lar thought repeatedly. Larry was shocked at what he'd just said. Marilyn was ready to make a deal; details were all that was left. *"Nah, it's good,"* thought Lar. *"This'll freak Simms and Johnson out. They'll not know what we're going to do."*

They pushed through while hands grabbed at Lar.

"What about the third shooter?"

"Have you heard from Stonek's attorneys?"

"When do you expect the trial to be?"

Lar thought, *"That last question—they're so stupid? They'll believe anything, repeat anything in groupthink; just say it and they'll believe it. People are so stupid, and television reporters are worse; they'll repeat anything."* They pushed to the elevator and rode down to the tunnel with a combination of reporters that thought he'd answer questions now and confused defendants and their families just trying to get out of the way. No answers here either.

As they finally escaped, alone, into the tunnel, Lacy, the old guy from the *Chronicle*, was waiting.

*"Aren't you afraid you'd miss something upstairs?"* They walked slowly by Lacy and toward the garage as Lacy leisurely picked up the pace and walked along.

"I didn't miss anything up there, did I," Lacy said—it wasn't a question.

*"Tons."*

"A little crazy?"

*"The only thing better than no reporters is too many of them. Either way, you don't have to answer any stupid questions."*

"How are you dealing with Simms?"

*"This is off the record."*

"Of course."

*"Good. Fine. We're having dinner tonight,"* Lar said. *"He's a little odd, but he works hard, and that works better for everyone."*

"Have you found a subject he's not an expert at?"

Lar laughed. *"No."*

"Slow down a sec; you're speeding up. Simms tried to explain to me why my last five articles were wrong."

*"He's thorough."*

"Not the facts—the writing." Lacy laughed.

*"What can I say?"*

"You going to take their deal." Lacy said it as a conclusion, his voice lowered to mark the gravity of his statement.

*"Not yet."* Lar counted on Lacy to break his word and ask Simms a question that would reveal to Simms the next bit of information. *"I may have a surprise yet."*

"Johnson's sweating it out. He doesn't have shit on Stonek. They arrested him too soon."

*"They got excited."*

"Carelessness. Johnson's boss thought it would be good headlines; they didn't consult Simms beforehand."

*"Yeah?"*

"Simms is like a maid over there; he's always cleaning up their messes."

They stopped and shook hands, and Lar said, *"Gotta go; he may not be able to this time."*

"Can I say you're still talking?" Lacy called to them as they walked away.

"Yeah," Lar said back as they entered the garage. *"Lacy would like that, makes him important,"* Lar thought.

As Lar drove out of the garage, his cell rang. It was Legs.

"We're not finished with this. We need to talk to you now."

That was fine with him. *"What's your name?"* Lar asked.

"Wiley."

*"No, your first."*

"Cheri."

*"Cheri,"* Lar said as he, alone now, drove to his downtown hotel. *"I'll meet with you if you want to argue with me."* He didn't care what she had to say, but he did want to confirm how desperate Cheri was for information on what he was up to and how ambitious she was to get it.

Lar lived at the nicest hotel downtown. He met Legs in the bar on the third floor overlooking Houston's city park, meant to duplicate New York's Central Park. It was a stereotypical bar for an expensive hotel: red-papered walls, western prints, and round furniture. Large flat-screens that were expected by the customers but clashed with the rest of the ambiance hung on the walls.

Lar shed his coat and tie, drank a whiskey and coke, and relaxed at a table looking down on the park. He drank and watched the women at the tables around him. He wasn't interested in anything the men were doing at the moment, and he thought about how to get Simms so involved in the Ramirez case that he didn't have time for anything else. Marilyn was eager to help him by pushing for a deal to get her case dismissed in return for testifying, but that alone wouldn't be enough; he needed more.

Lar watched Wiley snake through the crowded bar toward him between tables packed too close together. *"She's frowning like she's trying to communicate that she's unhappy with my lack of cooperation, like I give a shit. She's not dealing with that pussy anymore,"* he thought.

She wore a dark little woman-lawyer suit hemmed above her knees and had awful square cropped hair. She had tight round hips that Lar thought might actually move when she walked if she'd relax a little.

"I told Mr. Ulm that you finally agreed to meet," she said in a stern voice as she walked up.

*"That's"*—he drew the word out—*"what we're doing."*

"Don't you think we could pick someplace to talk privately? Your speech outside the courtroom and indiscretion were very unprofessional," she said, still standing.

*"Sit down; we'll move when we get down to business."*

She sat on the other side of the little round bar table, took a breath, and acted as if she might relax. He obviously wasn't going to work until they'd had a drink, so she might as well get on with it. "I'll have a martini," she told the waitress.

*"So, Cheri,"* Lar said, *"it's nice to meet you."*

"We met the night Mr. Ulm hired you, or rather, Mr. Ulm hired you for Miss Ramirez," she said.

*"Yeah, I know, but we were both busy doing what Ulm told us that night, and tonight we're not."*

"You're obviously not. I wonder if you ever have," she said. The waitress set her drink down. Legs sipped it. "But I still am."

*"I know. Where'd you go to law school? When did you graduate?"* He veered the conversation away from Ulm and what she needed to know.

"Two years ago I graduated from Vanderbilt." She allowed the subject to change. They talked about her and wherever that led; he didn't remember from one sentence to the next. He just kept the drinks coming and the conversation away from what she came to find out. Ulm must be desperate to know what Ramirez was going to do, because Legs wasn't leaving or even acting impatient yet. He knew Ulm worked for Stonek. Lar performed for the news cameras as much as for Ulm and his client, Johnson, and Simms. Maybe not Simms; he wouldn't bite on it. Lar could have gone out the back of the courtroom but he wanted to create panic, and he must have gotten it right because here she was, having drinks, letting her skirt creep up, and talking like she gave a shit what he said.

He allowed himself to be fooled into having two more drinks with her until she insisted on bringing the conversation to Ramirez and what she wanted to do. Legs was slurring her words and took her coat off. She wore a thin white silk blouse and leaned over the table as she talked, treating him like a date.

*"You said it's too crowded here now,"* Lar said when she asked, and she suggested they go upstairs so they could discuss the case in privacy. They had one more drink before they left the increasingly crowded and loud bar; she took a glass of champagne with her, and she insisted on getting away from all the eyes.

When they got to the suite, he hung their coats up and mixed another drink. No woman had been here since Larry leased this place after he got out of the hospital. Lar had had enough of Larry wasting time waiting on Diane's forgiveness; he needed sex. Legs obviously needed information desperately to take to Ulm, but she wasn't getting it.

"Mr. Lamb, I need…"

*"Larry,"* Lar thought; he hated that name. Weak. But you don't say what you're thinking, ever, so he'd stay with that name for now.

"Larry," she said, "what are you going to do?" She took her shoes off.

*"Good, she thinks she knows why we're up here,"* Lar thought. She wasn't wearing hose. Women, even many older professional women, don't wear hose in Houston; it's too hot. She could leave, but she wouldn't—couldn't—without the information she had to have, so their purposes intersected at sex, and without foreplay or even talking about it, they quickly shed their clothes and moved to the bed.

As he covered her body with his, her round hips moved rhythmically as she wrapped her legs around him. She pulled his hungry mouth to her warm neck and moaned as he entered her. Lar noticed she looked at him with calculating eyes in the middle of sex. He'd change that look, he thought, as they rocked.

She looked surprised as he pulled out and rose to his knees. He grabbed her hips and rolled her over. She growled, "No." The more she fought, the more excited and forceful he became. She grabbed a pillow and put it against the headboard and held on tight. His thrusts came harder and faster; her outcries multiplied his excitement.

He lowered himself to her ear and panted, *"I'm not telling what I'm going to do; I'm not telling you shit. Tell Ulm that."*

She shoved up like she was doing a marine push-up. "You fuckin' bastard, get off me." She bucked hard to get him off, but he held her fast until he finished.

She fought from under him. "Fucker," she yelled as she slammed the door when she left.

*"Yes, I am; yes, I am."*

# CHAPTER 15

"How long am I going to have to go to prison?" Marilyn asked. At Lar's insistence, she was allowed to change into her own clothes— a linen pantsuit; he'd rather have seen her in a skirt, but Marilyn looked good in anything other than her orange overalls. She'd been brought over to the police station by deputies, and she walked into the basement questioning dungeon; the police called it a questioning room, but it was a real dungeon. She walked in like she owned the building, proud and happy to see him. As their eyes met, her look told him that she knew Larry and Lar were both there and that she knew Lar was in charge.

"I'm ready; let's make a deal," she said when they were alone.

*"No; everyone's ready to fold—give me a little more time."* Lar needed Simms more involved in this to keep him too busy for the Bain investigation.

Simms came in alone, jacket on and tie tight against his collar, stepping robotically. "Can I talk to you outside, Mr. Lamb?" He twitched his mustache.

Marilyn smiled. "You don't have to protect me, Detective." She tasted the last word. "I won't get confused or upset; I didn't the last time we talked."

Whatever Marilyn tasted didn't affect Simms as he sat down unchanged across from her and Lar. They were next to each other, thighs barely touching, within each other's space, where they wanted to be, and Lar was confident of his poker hand. Simms gently slid some papers out of the case he carried and laid them flat on the table for her to read.

Simms said flatly as he stared into her eyes to read her reaction, "This is your agreement to testify at the trial of Donald Stonek, to give us a statement against him, and to fully cooperate with the State of Texas in the prosecution of him. Failure to fully cooperate will make this agreement void, and you will receive the maximum sentence."

She didn't look down at it or over to Lar; she just stared back with the ends of her mouth barely turned up. "How much?"

"Two years."

"*Dismiss,*" Lar said, finally drawing Simms's eyes away from studying Marilyn. Good; that's what Lar wanted to do.

"We agreed two years," Simms said to Lar.

"*No, we didn't. We're not doing it for anything other than dismiss.*"

Simms looked at him, shook his head like he'd made a decision, and pulled a second file from his case. "Fine, but Johnson said he had to have a deal by tomorrow, so I prepared a deal with dismiss just in case, but if she doesn't testify that he helped plan the attempted murder of his wife…"

"No problem there." Her full lips spoke, and Lar turned to watch them. Simms listened, but seemed not to be possessed by her. Lar was impressed because he'd never seen another man who wasn't overcome when she spoke directly to them. "It was Don's idea. Even those stupid wigs and names—how do you think I knew where she'd be all the time to tell those idiots? He even found them for me; I don't know how. They made my skin crawl."

"You'll have to write down a complete statement and sign it," Simms said.

Marilyn signed the agreement and then gave a long recorded statement to one of Simms's assistants. By the time they were done, Johnson arrived to look over the statement.

Afterward, out in the hall, Lar asked the DA about bond now that they had a deal.

Johnson answered, "She's not out until Stonek's in for good."

By that afternoon, Johnson leaked to the old newspaper columnist Lacy that Ramirez agreed to testify. Lar knew the instant Johnson's leak hit the

Internet because ten reporters left messages. He didn't answer those calls; they were too stupid to talk to and couldn't be of any service. Lacy's message did catch his attention as he left: "This is Doug Lacy. Ulm said his client is confident his credibility will overcome anything your client makes up to get off." Then, after a long pause, he concluded, "She's getting dismissed? Call me back and help me understand—are you double-crossing Ulm?"

Hell, yeah, Lar double-crossed everyone and got away with it. He'd made the deal, his terms. Larry couldn't make this deal. He'd made a deal at two, hell, five years. *Larry's weak and a dumbass, just like Simms. No, Simms is no dumbass—that's the problem; he's smart,* Lar thought. Lar had to keep him busy. Lar tightened the sash on his white hotel robe and sat on his balcony, finishing his coffee and watching the morning go by—and thinking. Yesterday had been a good day, but Simms wasn't busy enough yet. He picked up the phone.

"Johnson," came the immediate answer.

*"Miss Ramirez won't be able to testify until she sees her previous statements and Simms's reports."*

"That's bullshit. We have a deal."

*"Yeah, yeah, but I need to go over her statements or Simms's report to prepare her."*

"That might take a few days."

*"Then get Simms on it. We're working on our statement, and we want to make sure our story doesn't interfere with you."*

"Yeah, Ulm already had his associates…" Johnson started.

*"Might be my girl,"* Lar thought.

"over here to get a copy of her statement," Johnson said.

*"They can't have that shit, even if you had it."*

"Yeah, I told them to get out of here." He paused and then said, "I need it, though; we need to get that finished."

*"Then get Simms busy, and I'll meet with my client and get it done,"* Lar said as he hung up. That was easy. He should be angry at Marilyn for lying from the start, but he could forgive it because she only lied to Larry, and he'd always done that. It was easy. Larry, whether he acknowledged

it or not, wanted to be lied to by Lar, by Marilyn, by everyone, including Diane.

On Lar's way to the jail, Diane called. "Where've you been?"

*"What do you mean where have I been? Haven't you listened to the news?"* He was driving the short distance through downtown, stopping every twenty feet for traffic.

"You haven't called the kids. They miss you," she said.

*"That hurt Larry, or what was left of him,"* thought Lar. And he wondered that it was strange that she worried about that now since it was she that refused to let him move back.

Lar was going to tell her off, but weak Larry's desire won. "Tell Danny and Katie I love them. Daddy's sorry he hasn't been able to come see them, but I will as soon as I can."

"You've changed, Larry," she accused him. "You're getting sick again. Larry, will you please go see your doctor? It's all this stress from this case, isn't it?"

That made Lar so mad, he could hardly prevent himself from saying, *"Larry's dead. I killed him. You killed him."* But he didn't—Larry's remnant wouldn't let him. "Don't worry about how I'm feeling," Larry was finally allowed to say.

"Larry," she said again. Lar wished she'd stop saying that. "If you're not going to go see him, I'm going to call him. I still love you, Larry. Danny and Katie still love you."

That made Lar even madder, but all he said was *"I've got to go, Diane. Tell Katie and Danny I love them."*

Inside the jail's yellow-painted lobby, where families pack in to wait for night visitation time, stood the old man, Lacy, all by himself, standing as if Lar knew he had an appointment to meet him right there. Lar could talk to Lacy because he meant nothing to Lar other than that Lacy was a tool to be used.

"You got a better deal than I thought you'd get—even thought possible," Lacy said. He wore an old dark suit, like he'd bought it at a suit warehouse place ten years ago. His cheap white dress shirt looked wrinkled and brown, and it was probably one of those crappy nonwrinkle versions. He wore black shoes that looked like they were made out of rubber. They stood there talking alone in the expansive waiting room, their soft words echoing. Lacy couldn't go any farther inside because the three layered security gates prevented anyone but attorneys from visiting this time of day.

*"I know I did. I kick ass."*

"When are you going to announce to the court the details?"

Lar saw Lacy open a door to make Simms's life a little more complicated, and he stepped through it. *"Off the record? You never saw me."*

"Yeah." Lacy paid attention.

*"Detective Simms has screwed this thing up. It's why we're going to get it dismissed."* That's good, but Lar didn't know where he was going with this. He was making it up as he spoke.

"You got the deal so she'd testify," Lacy said cynically.

*"For a dismissal, Johnson offered ten years."*

"How'd Simms screw it up?"

How would he say? He didn't need to make that up; he'd just leave it at something and spread it around from there. First Lacy, then other reporters asking questions and getting in the way might keep Simms so busy he couldn't do anything else, like check into Bain's suicide, and if the publicity of questions got hot enough, maybe a politician or two might get nervous enough to call for some type of inquiry or investigation, and then Simms might get buried. *"Gotta go,"* he said, and he clicked his way through the first security gate and left.

"Now what?" Marilyn asked. They sat next to each other in the box. Marilyn had just finished rereading the statement they wrote outlining the plan Stonek suggested and that Marilyn and Stonek executed together.

Larry, if he'd been here, would've believed it completely. But Lar knew the truth was just as close to a romance novel as it was to her statement, but he didn't care. No matter what it said, it was getting her out of jail, and the crazier the better because that would confuse Simms and make him work more on Marilyn's case to figure out the truth, like there was any truth. Who knows what happened, what the facts were? He doubted anyone knew all the facts except Marilyn, and she used facts and truth like cards—she played some, she held others.

He knew she manipulated this case, her deal, even him, for her own intentions that he could not discern, but he didn't care about that either—that was for her. He had his own reasons to make this all as big a clusterfuck as he could, and besides, he wanted Marilyn out of jail. As it was going now, he was here, not Larry, not ever again, and Marilyn's power over others promised they could have a lot of fun together.

*"Now we turn this in to Johnson and read our deal in court,"* he said.

She looked at him as if she knew whom she spoke to, and Lar thought she did. As if she heard his thoughts, she said, "I like the way you are now; I think I'd like to get to know this you when I get out."

Of course she'd say that—that's Marilyn. She's like the God of Wind that likes to move the tide this way, then that, because it's the way she wants it, or just to do it for the enjoyment of the power to move everything, or everybody, in front of her.

*"We'll have all the time you want, but it'll have to wait awhile. Stonek's trial won't be for months, and you'll be stuck in prison until then."*

Marilyn smiled. "You just get this deal closed. It'll be sooner than you think."

*"You know it's Stonek's money Ulm gave me to represent you. They gave me research and information all along, but I told them yesterday to go screw themselves."*

"Did you get paid?"

*"I got enough."*

"Good; then we don't need 'em anymore."

Lar could smell her, just a clean soap smell, but since it was from her as she sat close, touched, it was perfume. They pretended to look at her statement together, but that's not why they sat so close, like teenagers. The fat guard didn't even pretend to look anymore.

"This case ruined me in Houston. We're going to have to change names and move—to Miami, maybe."

That wouldn't do; Lar had to stay here and make sure the world he built stayed together, and undiscovered, but he didn't want to lose his new gem either. *"Let's not assume that yet, Marilyn. You're going to be a celebrity, a star, when you get out, and I'm going to be the hottest criminal defense attorney in Texas, maybe the whole country."*

She twisted her waist and faced him square-shouldered. "What are you trying to feed me?" She smiled.

*"I'm not trying to con you; just don't get in such a hurry. This is going to be fun. Don't you want to enjoy being famous?"* Infamous, but it would feel the same to her, and they could enjoy it the same way.

They talked about her statement for a while, but she hesitated to sign it because then their meeting would be over. So they talked about food, where they'd eaten in town, and where they'd like to travel to. It all would have sounded like they were really falling for each other to anyone listening—it did to Larry—but Lar knew Marilyn was too good at her game to really feel anything. It was her smoke until she got out, gained control, and figured out what to do next. He also knew that if he could control her, at least control which way she broke in the chase, much like a cheetah does chasing an antelope, he could manipulate her to do as he desired. Lar knew Marilyn was thinking the exact same thing—how to manipulate them into doing what she wanted—and that's the other reason he wanted to be with Marilyn: she was like him. Not Larry, of course, but he was almost gone now anyway.

Lar looked at his watch, startled at how long they had talked, and he said, *"I've got to go. Chris is going to be off work before I can deliver your statement."*

"I can't believe you like that dwarf."

*"He's not a dwarf; he's not short. "* Lar laughed as they stood up, scraping chairs.

"No, he's a tall dwarf. He looks like a dwarf, and he's against me."

*"Only because he's got a job to do."*

"No," she said. "No, he's like Simms. I don't work with them."

Lar knew just what she meant. Marilyn controlled almost everyone around her, especially men. Larry felt it the first time he met her. When he was away from her, he was disgusted by her lying and not swayed by her average looks, but then she'd walk into a conference room and Larry forgot even who he was. That had helped Lar escape, again, but she didn't affect the detective or seem to reach the assistant district attorney. Neither Lar nor Marilyn knew why not, but it didn't matter. Despite Larry, Lar negotiated a deal that got all her charges dismissed for testifying against Stonek, who'd go to prison as they went on vacation. Lar liked that.

*"That Simms and Johnson are beyond your control doesn't matter anymore, Marilyn—we won,"* he said as she left to return to her cell. They looked into each other's eyes, her pale, pale blue eyes; he'd never really seen them this way before, and he wanted to kiss her, but he couldn't, not here, not now, and then she disappeared behind the steel doors as he headed to the DA.

The next morning, standing in the middle of the courtroom in front of the bench, surrounded by deputies ordered to maintain the court's decorum and next to the district attorney and Marilyn, Lar was ready to announce the deal his client had made with the State of Texas in exchange for her testimony against Donald Stonek. The courtroom benches were packed with attorneys, spectators, tourists, and reporters. Attorneys from all over the courthouse crowded the jury box and all the standing room allowed. When he'd initially walked into the back of the courtroom, done to avoid the riot of television cameras in the hallway, he entered like a winning gladiator. Other attorneys wanted to talk to him. Defendants pled for his card, and reporters wanted to have their picture made with him for their blogs. Johnson frowned at Lar's popularity at his expense. "Larry, can we get this done?"

*"Larry. Larry. That sheep wasn't here anymore. He was dead,"* thought Lar.

Johnson told one of the five bailiffs—any other day there'd only be one in the courtroom—to bring out Miss Ramirez. Lar and Johnson announced the deal to the judge, who accepted it after asking Miss Ramirez a few questions to ensure that it was her agreement. Lar noticed Marilyn working the judge. Once she was before him, looking into his face, answering him, the judge's attitude turned—perceptible only to ones watching for it—from acting tough in front of reporters and angry at the storm in his courtroom (and the effect that the notoriety of the case would have on his political future) to a nuanced, softer manner. It reminded Lar of vanilla ice cream.

Chris saw it, too, and as the bailiffs escorted Marilyn back to her cell and the two stood apart from the mass of people for just the briefest of moments, he said, "Well, that sucked. Guess if she blows the deal, I'll have to try to get another judge." They both grinned at each other, but before Lar responded, they were buried by people. The judge banged his gavel and shouted for the bailiffs to silence the courtroom. Lar and Chris escaped out the back exit and down the secured judge's private hall.

"*What's next?*" Lar asked. He truly didn't know. He'd never done any of this before, and he no longer had Legs to brief him.

"I ask the court to revoke Stonek's bond, and we go to trial. Time to go to war," Chris said as he turned into a room and shut the door.

Lar slipped down the private elevator and out of the courthouse.

# CHAPTER 16

The newspaper headlines read, "Ramirez Turns On Lover" and "Stonek Taken Back Into Custody."

The next few days the publicity about the case made Lar feel like he was standing in the middle ring at the circus. Reporters had his number now, which made his cell phone useless again. Even if someone wanted to contact him, it couldn't be done. He had to turn his phone off unless he was making a call. Marilyn suggested he buy a burner. Hotel security kept anyone from getting to his suite—or most anyone—and the front desk refused to take any messages. His office was buried with calls and reporters showing up in the mistaken belief he ever went there. None of it mattered; he had what he wanted—chaos.

Marilyn's statement said Stonek directed her in hiring his wife's murderers, told her who to use, how to contact them, and the most damning evidence, supplied her with the money for cars, guns, and the killers.

"Miss Ramirez is obviously selling her soul to escape her sole responsibility for these terrible attacks on Mrs. Stonek." *"How did Ulm become such a big-time lawyer?"* Lar wondered. *"He was a terrible liar and a worse speaker in front of the cameras."* Ulm's reputation was so big, though, that the press didn't seem to notice. Anyone watching would assume Stonek might get off if Ulm was representing him. And it made Lar's—Larry's—reputation just as big, because he was going to win. The public would think they saw Larry win and Ulm lose, but Larry wasn't who would win—Lar was.

Lar thought again about changing his name, at least to some other version of Lawrence, since he wasn't really Larry and was tired of others calling him Larry. Larry was almost dead now, and he only came out when

Lar needed him, like when that fucking Simms started nosing around. Lar? L? There wasn't another name; it was Lawrence or Larry. Maybe he could go by Lamb; that would be ironic.

As Lar sat on his balcony hidden from the crowds, he enjoyed his new routine of letting the morning sun warm his face as he sipped coffee in his robe. He heard the local television news playing in his den and echoing through his suite. His laptop sat next to him loaded into TOR and moving his newly liquid funds to untraceable locations. He felt like Napoleon when he blew the nose off the sphinx with a cannon shot; there was nothing he could not do. He enjoyed relishing his triumphs.

Lar was jarred back to reality when his suite phone rang—unusual because the hotel didn't allow any calls through. The front desk clerk said a Detective Simms called and that the police needed to see him immediately.

When Lar stepped out of the elevator from the garage at the police headquarters lobby, a screaming mob of reporters stampeded him.

"What's happening?" he asked.

"The word is your client has new charges."

Lar was surprised, and he wondered what Marilyn got caught doing now. He knew she was still up to something, but he expected her to wait until at least he got her out of jail before she tried anything else, not that she'd ever really tell him what she'd do. *"I'm just here to check a file. I don't know why you're here. There's nothing,"* he said. The panicked herd shoved him back and forth as he pretended to try to get through. This was too good to rush, but Larry was scared.

"A source leaked that she was caught passing something to another prisoner."

"Can we expect a statement?"

"Are you scheduled to appear in court on these new charges?"

As Lar slowly worked his way through the reporters and cameramen, he smiled and posed for their pictures. *"Guys, I don't know what you're talking about. No one called me. I'm just here to check some files."* The crowd parted and stopped as he entered through police security and then went up the elevator to see Simms.

Lar walked into Simms's office already talking. *"What's the emergency? The reporters in the lobby said you filed new charges against Miss Ramirez?"*

Johnson stood next to Simms's desk, his coat off, tie loose, face red, hands swinging. "That stupid, stupid bitch. She's crazy. Crazy. I shoulda never made a deal with you." He slammed his Styrofoam cup of coffee down on Simms's desk, bursting it and splashing coffee over the jumbled papers covering Simms's messy desk. He didn't notice, but walked by Lar and out of the office saying, "It's all shit now. I'm fucked, and fuck you."

That upset Larry, but Lar knew it was about business, and Johnson would get over it, whatever it was, or not—he didn't care. *"What's going on? What's he so upset about?"* Lar said as Simms pulled an old towel from his desk and tried to save his papers. Lar eased into a chair and waited, enjoying watching Simms jerk up papers and wipe them off trying to save his work. *Screw Simms; any small mess of his was worth enjoying.*

"We haven't filed new charges against Ramirez—yet."

*"What'd she do? She's been stuck in jail; it's not like she could do anything."* *Not until she got out.*

Simms sat down hard in his large desk chair and took a deep breath to ease his tension and bring his mind to the moment. "She got caught passing a note to another prisoner."

*"Big deal."*

"It is a big deal. She tried to hire someone to kill Donald Stonek."

Lar couldn't breathe; his heart stopped. Of all the things Marilyn could have done, of all the schemes he expected her to be planning, killing Donald Stonek was not one of them. He didn't respond, but concentrated on maintaining his poker face.

"Yeah." Simms laughed, "You didn't expect that move either." Simms was reading Lar's body language. "Kind of fucked all our days up. I tell you, she's one step ahead of me on this one. I didn't expect this at all."

Lar gathered himself back together, suppressed Larry's panic, and said, *"Are you sure? Did you get the note, or is this just some word of another prisoner?"* He had to find out what they had.

"Oh, we've got the note. Wish we didn't. We can't ignore it. Johnson has to tell Stonek's attorneys. This is going to totally screw everything up."

*"Can I see it? What happened?"*

"She passed a note to one of her buddies in the jail; it said she needed to get someone to kill her boyfriend. Her pal was getting out today; I guess Ramirez thought she might need a job." Simms handed Lar a copy of a scribbled note; it was Marilyn's writing, and it did say she needed someone to kill Donald Stonek. "Right while they were eating supper."

That was awfully careless of Marilyn—too careless. Lar knew she was reckless; the laughable attempts on the sweet wife's life proved that. They were never quite planned out enough. She picked idiots that couldn't get the job done, and at least in the first two attempts, they didn't have an escape plan. The first shooter hid in the woods waiting for a bus. At least Marilyn's latest explosion would keep Simms busy. Lar had no idea whether it was true, but he said, *"That's not enough; even if she wrote it, writing that down isn't against the law by itself."* Simms didn't respond, and Lar thought that was a good enough sign to continue, *"Hell, you've done such a good job in the Ramirez case, I might have written that about you."*

"If you'd done it, you'd been interfering with the police," Simms joked.

*"But she didn't; you said she just handed it to another prisoner—that doesn't prove anything."* Lar liked his argument, but he wished Simms hadn't made the joke.

"Well, it sure destroys our case against Stonek. She doesn't have any credibility now. She can't try to kill him if he's her lover and coconspirator in his wife's murder."

*"Why not? I'll still get her to testify; she'll keep her deal."*

"Bet you will, but it won't matter what she'll do; it screws the case against Stonek."

So she did it on purpose, Lar realized; she must have planned it before she made the deal. The revelation almost knocked Lar out of control.

"And I doubt you've any idea what she'll do next," Simms said.

Lar didn't hear him; he was thinking of his own delusions. He thought he controlled Marilyn just as he had taken control of Larry, hidden in his little dark place now, but she must have been in control after all. She manipulated the agreement and then intentionally got caught passing a note that would destroy her credibility. Now she'd go free and so would Stonek.

Lar liked that, even if he was used as a tool. She'd make a great partner once she was free unless her double-dealing wasn't finished and she also intended to reconnect with Stonek. He stood up to leave, and Simms said, "Don't go yet; I'm not finished."

*"I think I need to talk to my client, don't you?"*

"I need to talk to you about Bain. I need some more help."

*"Call me later. You're about to charge my client with more charges. No telling what's she's hearing. I'm sure she's in a panic at her mistake, if it's true."* He knew none of what he said was.

"No; sit down," Simms said.

A young detective in a cheap gray suit from Sears and black, slicked-back hair like a Baptist preacher stepped in with an expression that said, "Sit down."

Lar turned on Simms and said, *"What's going on? Are you interfering with me consulting with my client? Detective, your case may be screwed, but you haven't made any mistakes; don't start now."* Lar was trying to give Simms an easy way to reconsider this move and let him go. Lar could smell this wasn't about Ramirez.

"I'm still not. Sit down."

They sat—Lar and now Larry, too. Simms grabbed another thick file, an old one. Sirens screamed in the far distance, mixed with the outside office noise. It was always there, but Larry could always hear it more than Lar.

*"What the fuck is this about?"* He knew as he said it, and then he gestured at the young guy and added, *"And who let their kid off the football team?"*

Simms dug new subfiles out of the pile of old ones and said, "I'm having some trouble about the last day Bain died."

*"We all are, and we appreciate you working so hard on it. I fought to get your force to, but don't you think we need to deal with the disaster first?"*

Simms looked up at them and put his file down on his desk. "You know, sometimes I hear politicians say 'we' on TV when they're speaking, but I know that's their own egotistical royal reference or something, but I never heard anybody use it like you do."

*"What the fuck are you talking about?"*

"I mean, just now, you said, 'We appreciate.' You do that all the time. I never heard someone say it like that."

*"What difference does that make? The biggest case in Houston just blew up, you're accusing my client of passing a note about killing Donald Stonek, and you're talking about this?"*

Apparently Simms wasn't too busy with his disaster to continue nosing around in Bain, and he thought he had something big enough to make them sit back down.

"You said you didn't go see Bain the day he died. Will you take a polygraph?"

*"What?"*

"Polygraph?"

Lar had him. *"Yeah, now, let's do it and get this nonsense over."* He'd let Larry take the test.

Simms watched through the one-way glass as Lamb answered the young officer's questions on the polygraph. Simms thought he had it figured out. After the first time talking to Lamb's doctor, he'd done some research on his own about duplicitous personality disorder. Then he called the doctor back, and the doctor quickly said, "Detective Simms, I'm glad you called."

"Why?"

"After we spoke a few days ago and you asked about anything Mr. Lamb said during a session about Bain, I remembered that in one session he'd muttered something about him."

"And?"

"I went back and listened, and in the recording he mentioned that he'd had to see Bain to end that problem."

"What problem?"

"I don't know. I didn't pay attention to just the one utterance, and nothing was ever mentioned again about it."

"Did he say when?"

"No, that's it. I wouldn't have told you even that, but Mr. Lamb was clear that I was supposed to help you in any way I could."

Then Simms got back to the reason he'd initially called. "Could Mr. Lamb have visited Bain to solve the problem and not known it?" It sounded stupid to ask that, but Simms had an idea after his own research.

"What do you mean?"

"I mean, could he have done it as one person, and the other not know it?"

"That type of psychosis is extremely rare. There have been incidental examples of disorders that severe, but I doubt Mr. Lamb could have done that since those symptoms disappeared so quickly. I wouldn't..."

Simms was impatient with the doctor's dropping back into his psychiatrist-examining-all-possibilities routine, and he said, "Could one of the personalities have hidden from you—instead of the symptoms just disappearing?" He spoke with derision at the doctor's naïveté.

"I doubt that. We'd find that over time."

"You didn't have time."

"No." The doctor paused like he was thinking about it. "No, we didn't."

After the test, Lamb stayed in the same room waiting on the report.

The kid took the test to Simms and said, "He passed. Man, that's a surprise."

"No, it's not," Simms corrected him. "Now, bring him back in."

"Well, are you satisfied? Can I get back to work?" Larry said as he checked his watch and stood. He knew he didn't go see Bain that last day and that he passed the test.

"No, not yet. Sit down, please. I need to ask you something."

Larry sat, and he really didn't mind. He was in control again, and though he was terrified at what was happening, he knew only parts, and he was relieved to be back.

"I believed you'd pass the test, Mr. Lamb."

"Then why'd you ask me to take it?"

Simms looked across his cluttered, messy desk into the eyes of Lamb, trying to discern whom he was looking at. "I had to make sure who I was talking to."

"What does that mean?"

Simms stayed silent for a few seconds instead of responding immediately, thinking how to say his next sentence. "Mr. Lamb, Mrs. Bain said Brian was waiting on you the day he was murdered."

"You've told me that before. I…"

"And you've said yourself that you went up there that day to fix a problem with Bain," Simms said. He knew that's not exactly what Lamb said, but he bet that's what Lamb did, so he said it.

"When'd I say that? I never said that."

"Yeah, you did, to Dr. Henderson during one of your counseling sessions right after you were admitted, about a week after Brian Bain was found dead."

Larry looked at him. He remembered checking into the hospital, he remembered counseling with Dr. Henderson, but he didn't remember ever saying that. How could he? It wasn't true. "No, I don't believe you. I didn't say that—it's not true."

Simms again let a few moments of silence go by while they looked at each other. More sirens—they sounded like ambulances this time—police officers talking loudly from one desk to another, muffled sounds. An officer stood outside the glass office talking to others nearby at their desks, but not moving.

"Maybe." Simms stopped, and then said, "It wasn't you."

"You just said I said it," Larry accused, but he shivered like an ice cube slid down his spine. Larry wondered, "Does Simms know about Lar? He couldn't. No one did. Marilyn knows. Dr. Henderson didn't." Larry never said anything to the doctor about it, but he didn't remember talking to him the first week he was in the hospital either. It seemed like it was two, maybe three, weeks before he had any counseling sessions with Henderson.

"Larry, are there times"—Simms drew out the last word—"that you don't remember what you've done or where you've been?"

"No," Lamb said quickly. "Do you think you're a psychiatrist? No, there's not, I'd remember if I saw Brian that day." Wouldn't he? Things were happening all the time now that he had no idea how they happened or where he'd been. It had happened today, but no, not that day. "Can I go? Either charge me with something or release me. I have to go talk to my client."

"Go. You've done what I asked."

Larry shoved the door open, pushed by the offensive lineman, and walked out of the station. He didn't think about anything until he was out in the dark night. The horde of reporters must have assumed he snuck out some other way and abandoned their stakeout. It was too late to see Marilyn tonight; he'd not realized how long he'd been in that fascist block until now: 10:00 p.m.

Lar stood at his hotel bar and ordered a Scotch. The place was full of businessmen—at the tables, the whole bar around him, even standing up in the empty spaces.

Larry was there with someone, too, as he leaned onto the bar staring at his drink. "What a cliché," he thought, "standing here, divorced guy, late at night, drinking his troubles." Lar thought it was just Larry's weakness and cowardice, and he drifted out of the dark shadow and assumed his place next to Larry. Seeing him, Larry ordered another Scotch.

*"What do you drink that shit for?"* Lar said.

"I like it."

*"No, you don't. You like bourbon."*

"I'm from Pennsylvania, not Texas; bourbon is too sweet," Larry yelled out loud.

"Excuse me, sir?" asked the bartender.

"Nothing." Larry didn't realize he'd said it out loud. "Sorry; talking to myself, someone."

"I understand," the bartender said as he walked down the bar and faded into the crowd and noise. The televisions blared basketball. Everyone around him but one laughed and yelled, but the noise faded in and out.

Now, it faded out. *"Time to get back into your hole, Larry,"* Lar said.

"Not yet."

*"Larry?"* Lar drew it out. *"You know you want to. You're safe there; go on."* And Lar drew out the last word again, pushing Larry to his hole.

Larry pushed back, fought it; he wouldn't yield yet—he had to know. "Did you go there?"

*"Did I go where?"* Lar pretended puzzlement as he looked around at the available women for a target.

"To Brian's?"

*"You don't want to know that, Larry. Don't look there; you don't want to know."*

"I've got to. Simms thinks I was."

*"You passed that test."*

"And you made sure I was the one that took it. I've got to know; I've got to know for…"—he breathed deep, expanding his lungs like he was a yoga instructor—"for Brian."

*"For Brian? Drama boy. Look at yourself. I'm in charge. You can't handle it out here. You're famous; you can have a different woman every night—sometimes I do. There's a couple of nice young things eyeing you in here right now, and you stand there and think 'for Brian.' Fuck him. You couldn't handle that shit; you were about to fuck it all up, but that's not what happened. He died—and you're a famous criminal attorney—for nothing. You didn't have to do shit, and it's a good thing, 'cause you couldn't. And we're finished with your drama tonight; I don't know if letting you out is worth the trouble."*

With Larry gone, Lar turned around, and there was a blonde, thirtyish, maybe fortyish, in a short skirt sitting at a table alone looking at him, just like he told Larry. Yes, he was famous.

# CHAPTER 17

**66** **W**hat the hell did you do?" Lar asked Marilyn when she sat down. He had a long night, a good night, but a long one to work out his tension, but it was still there. When he woke up, he had more than the blonde in his bed to deal with; he had Marilyn and Simms. He got rid of the blonde and rushed to the jail.

"It's eleven in the morning; I expected you before now."

*"I didn't finish with Simms till late last night."*

"And you slept in? With who? I'm jealous." She moved next to him, acting like she was cuddling.

*"I know how jealous you really are."*

"Oh, I know who I'm talking to today—good."

*"You sit much closer, and you'll be in my lap."*

"Complaining?"

*"No, but you might finally make that pig out there do his job."* Lar jerked his head in the direction of the unseen guard.

"Don't worry about him; he just wants to make me happy."

*"That's what everyone wants to do, isn't it—make you happy?"*

"Aren't we nasty today?"

*"Did you plan on doing it all along?"*

"No, of course not. I was just upset and did something stupid." She answered too quickly, and that meant "yes."

*"Come on, Marilyn."* He drew out her name. *"I'm your lawyer; tell me the truth."* Lar already knew it.

"I thought you were a lot more than my lawyer."

"*That's what I am today.*"

"She must have been better last night than usual."

"*That's not working. Are you coordinating this with Stonek? How are you communicating with him?*"

"I'm not. I told you, I just got upset and did something stupid. I never meant it."

Lar laughed. "*You can be such a bad liar when you want to.*"

"I don't want to…wait, what do you mean?"

"*I mean, you set this up to get off and still get Stonek off. And I know it, and you really don't care that I know it. All I want to know is how you're coordinating it with Stonek.*"

"I'm not; I didn't."

Lar knew she denied it just so she wouldn't have to answer any more of his questions. How long she planned it, was this the plan all along if they got caught, and what part Stonek had in the plan were all questions he wanted to ask but didn't; she'd lie anyway. This was so perfectly timed, so completely perfect in its execution, that Lar didn't believe Marilyn could have done it all by herself. She'd been in charge of Mrs. Stonek's murder attempts, and not one succeeded—the first two didn't even have escape plans. Dumbass. It disgusted Lar. It wasn't hard to kill somebody, and it wasn't hard getting away with it. The only murders the cops solved were the ones where someone admitted shit to somebody; they couldn't figure anything out on their own. Murder was easy, except with fuckwads like Simms. He was a problem. "*So, when you get out, is it me or Stonek?*"

Marilyn looked at him like the question never occurred to her, that the very need to ask the question hurt her, and that the answer was obvious. "You—you know the answer." Then she smiled to joke, "But if you stay this nasty, I may change my mind."

Lar thought, "*She may anyway, even if she's telling the truth, but that's OK, too.*" Her sauce was worth the trouble, and it was especially perfect sauce to Lar, and that was a good thing, since she was constant trouble. "*OK, no more shit then. You've done what you meant to do—no more.*"

"Of course not. I'm not going to lose my head again."

*"She's sticking to her story,"* he thought. *"We have a hearing in the morning, so I'll see you then."*

"Am I getting out tomorrow?"

That surprised Lar. She thinks this is going to move even faster than he does. She must be talking to Legs or Miller—but how in jail? He didn't care; it's done now.

*"No—we'll see what happens. I expect the DA's head to explode."*

"Good."

*"You'd like him. He's smart and young and good-looking, just one of the types you prey on most."*

"I don't need the dwarf, do I?"

As they stood to part, he said, *"No, you don't."*

She looked at him. "Soon, when you leave me, I can kiss you good-bye."

*"We've always felt like you did anyway."*

"We?" Marilyn stopped and asked, "Larry back?"

*"No, he's still back there, somewhere, safe."* Lar joked, *"I just meant you always had him twisted."*

She whispered to pretend it was a secret. "It's what I do."

He whispered back, "I know." And then he left.

They didn't know what they did the rest of the day or who was in charge. Larry was never in charge anymore unless Lar allowed it, and Lar was inactive because of his freezing panic that Simms knew about him and what he'd done. That damn doctor. Fuck him for telling Simms. But Larry gave his complete approval for the doctor to tell Simms about his medical history because Larry didn't know either. Dumbass. Larry was always a dumbass—about his wife, about himself; that's why he wasn't in charge anymore.

They found themselves awake the next morning getting ready for Marilyn's court hearing—Simms was going to be there, too. Simms. Simms. What the hell was he going to do about Simms? In the tunnel on the way to the building, Lacy waited—old man. He was too old to get in the riot upstairs, and too smart. He wore a crappy, old, dark blue suit and a trench coat—what a stereotype.

Lar said as he walked up to him, *"Why you all dressed up? New suit? Are you going to be interviewed by one of the TV stations on your observations of the case? Why aren't you upstairs where the action is?"*

"'Cause I'd miss you," Lacy said with his cigarette voice.

*"I have to go through there."*

"No, you don't. You found the back way out last time; you won't fight that pack of poodles again."

*"They're that smart?"*

"Probably."

They shook hands and walked to the elevator together. "I hear you took a lie detector test?"

That gave them heartburn. Of course this old man heard that. He talked to everyone, had for years. He was not like these lazy TV reporters with their good hair.

*"Yeah, off the record."*

"You're not going to deny it?" Lacy said with a little humor in his crusty voice.

*"Nah, not to you; you know your shit."*

"What was it about?"

*"So you don't know everything."*

"I know attorneys don't agree to lie detectors with the police on cases they're working on."

*"You went to law school to know that?"*

"I'll write it if I get a confirmation on what it's about."

Lar couldn't have that, but he couldn't show his fear of it either. The old guy knew mentioning his hidden card—that he'd write about it— would get the play he wanted.

Lar gave in. *"It's on the old Bain case. They just needed to exclude me from what happened. It was a box-checking thing, so of course I'm going to help. I had begged them to keep looking into that for months."*

"Bain? That's closed."

"*It was.*"

Lacy smiled and knowingly said, "That's Simms, isn't it? That know-it-all can't let anything go. He opened it, I bet, just to show the other detectives all the mistakes they made."

This piqued Lar's interest. So, Simms wasn't popular with his coworkers either. He thought he'd test it. *"Who told you about the test?"*

"No one...someone."

*"It wasn't someone to help Simms."*

"No, no, it wasn't one of his friends."

Thank you. *"Gotta go."*

When Lar walked into the back of the courtroom, it was packed like the crowd expected a celebrity, and they had. Donald Stonek sat with his team of attorneys. Reporters sat or stood where they were allowed, quietly trying to overhear what was being said. Twenty attorneys unconnected to the case, but who happened to be at the courthouse and could slip by the bailiff, stood around the file table to watch what was going to happen. Johnson in a dark suit and expensive gator black cowboy boots huddled with four other assistant DAs at his table. He nodded at Lar with a grin like he was glad to see him, but Lar knew this poker face.

*"Your boyfriend's here,"* he told Marilyn in the holding cell. Usually the cell was full for morning hearings, but apparently the judge canceled all the other hearings and was only hearing their case. Not good.

"It's going to be fun this morning," she said through the glass.

She'd been talking to someone again.

*"Johnson's going to tell the judge about your little accident."*

"He doesn't watch the news?"

*"Johnson's making it official."*

"Bet Don's lawyer asks for a dismissal."

Yeah, she's talking. *"I'll ask the bailiff to bring you out early."*

"Thanks."

Lar reentered the courtroom. The judge still wasn't on the bench; it was nine fifteen, and he should have been out fifteen minutes ago. As Lar stepped over Johnson's huddle toward his own table, Donald Stonek looked through his gang of attorneys eye to eye and shook his head, "hello." It told Lar that Stonek wasn't worried. Ulm saw it and looked over to see who Stonek was looking at and then turned back to his minions like Lar was just another attorney in the courtroom. Legs, on the other side of Ulm, peered through the pack at Lar with hate in her eyes, and then she too disappeared back into the pack. She looked nice—too bad that bridge was burned.

"Your client's as dirty as they get," Johnson said as he walked up.

"*Yeah, I know—makes me look like a fool*," Lar said like he actually cared.

"Ulm's team's moving for dismissal. They've already given me the motion."

"*I expected that. This judge isn't going to grant that; he'll let you get to trial. He doesn't want all those voters watching the news to hear that he let Stonek off.*"

"That's just it. After your client screwed me, I can't hold him to trial. I'm fucked. I have no witness worth a shit now."

"*She'll testify. She'll keep her deal.*"

"Fine for her, but her testimony that she is in love with Stonek and they planned it together is totally discredited now that she's trying to kill him. I'm going to have to dismiss charges, and I know they planned this shit. It pisses me off, but the case is gone."

"*Bailiff?*" Lar turned to the deputy. "*Can you bring my client into the courtroom?*"

The big deputy, angrily staring at the crowded courtroom's disarray, said, "As soon as the judge comes in and gives me permission."

The courtroom doors opened, and Lar turned to see what the roar from the hallway released. Mrs. Stonek walked in, surrounded by private guards. Ulm rushed over and guided her to a front-row seat, the whole time whispering in her ear as she nodded to whatever he was saying. In a scene that could not have been staged better, she looked at her husband as they spoke into each other's ears. The reporters in the courtroom went wild asking questions, and the deputy barked at them to get quiet or get out. Mrs. Stonek took her seat with an air of someone who was well-aware of her social position and the media coverage she was getting.

Lar saw Simms watching him, and they briefly locked looks. Lar turned to take a seat while he waited for the judge to come in, and Ulm touched his arm and whispered close to his ear, where just they could hear, "You've done a good job, Lamb. You know, you made me mad as hell when you cut my team off, but you've done a great job representing Ramirez." He offered his hand, smiling. Lar couldn't discern what this smile meant. It might just be like a crocodile that looks like it's always smiling. It might be for the reporters in the audience and peeking through the door. It didn't matter.

They shook hands. *"Thanks. It's turning out a little different than I thought though. I know you're happy about that."*

"I am. It all works out, and your client's going free no matter what happens, so I know you don't care."

Yes, he does care if Stonek goes free. Lar didn't truly trust which one Marilyn would choose. He could feel Simms behind him still looking at him, studying him.

"All stand," another bailiff shouted, and the black-robed, white-haired old judge slid into his chair on the bench.

"Be seated," the judge said.

Lar heard the shuffling of the packed crowd all trying to squeeze down as he sat. Ulm sat in a chair in front that Legs reserved for him at their defense table. As Lar glanced to watch, she gave him another look of disgust and then looked back to the judge.

"Bring the defendant in," Judge Vack said. Two bailiffs walked her in, and as she stepped into the courtroom, she looked out on the full audience, looked at Mrs. Stonek sitting in the front row behind her husband, and then to Donald Stonek himself. She strutted unafraid, like all was going as she intended. She should have looked on this room, with all her known opponents and accomplices, except the two captured shooters that without any real legal representation pled guilty and received more than ten years each in prison without any hope or chance, like a craps table with the dice still rolling, but her expression was more like a card dealer that knew the hands of all the players before she dealt them. The bailiffs sat her next to Lar.

Lar apparently wasn't the only one to read this on her face either. He'd heard Johnson grumble as soon as he saw her. Johnson was incredibly intelligent, if not also extremely cynical, and was annoyed and angry she'd won at his expense. He would have to answer to his superiors about this manipulation. Lar was sure that Chris's suspicions were as strong as his own—Stonek was behind this scandal. It was too perfect to be executed by anyone else involved in the case. Lar also knew Chris wouldn't have to answer many, if any, questions from reporters about the specifics. Most of them were too lazy or stupid to figure out what happened, except for Lacy.

As she sat, Marilyn saw Detective Simms studying her attorney, and then she noticed Mrs. Stonek looking over at her. As soon as they caught each other's eyes, Mrs. Stonek looked back at her husband with a trusting expression.

*"Gives you faith in marriage, doesn't it?"* Lar said.

"Completely. Just like my faith in justice today," she said.

Over the last few days, Mrs. Stonek gave several television interviews, in which she proclaimed her husband's innocence and her utter disbelief that there was any way he could have been involved in the attempts on her life. All she wanted was to help her husband get this behind him so they could get on with their private lives together. She said she'd been proven right to believe in her husband's innocence when Ramirez tried to have him killed too, and she didn't care what happened to that vile woman.

Lar leaned over to Marilyn and whispered, *"She must really love the money. She's doing a great job, don't you think?"*

"She's a crack addict." Marilyn smiled.

*"So are you."*

"Maybe." She turned to face him. "But I don't need that marshmallow." They stared at each other for a fraction of a second, not as lovers or even people that cared for each other, but as two gunslingers, each trying to read if the other one was about to draw.

"Mr. Johnson," the judge said.

Johnson stood up, while the other three DAs remained seated. "Yes, Your Honor."

"Are you ready to proceed?"

Ulm stood up as he waited for Johnson's announcement.

"Yes, Your Honor."

"I take it we're dealing with Mr. Ulm's client first," the judge said as he looked at Ulm standing. Lar wondered if he shouldn't have talked to Johnson more about the hearing before it started, or at least shown up earlier, but it didn't matter; the results were preordained. He could feel Simms still looking at him.

"Yes, Your Honor. The state moves to dismiss the charges at this time," Johnson said, straight-faced, without a sign of how angry he was.

"Mr. Ulm?"

"I request that my client be released from bond at this time," Ulm said.

"Granted."

The DA was finished with Marilyn now, and it was time for her to go free.

Lar stood up.

The judge said, "Our next case is Ramirez versus the State of Texas. State, are you ready to proceed?"

"Yes, Your Honor."

"Mr. Lamb, are you ready to proceed?"

*"Yes, Your Honor,"* Lar said.

"Mr. Johnson," the judge said as he nodded at the DA.

"Your Honor, pursuant to the agreement, the State moves to dismiss the charges against Miss Ramirez."

"Your Honor, I request the defendant be released at this time." Lar said.

"No, she'll have to go back to the jail. They have to process her out, but she'll be out by the end of the day," the judge said, and then he turned to the DA. "Granted, Mr. Johnson. Do you have anything else before this court?"

"No, Your Honor."

"Then this court is adjourned for the morning." The judge popped his gavel, and then he quickly stood up and slipped out his back door that went to his chambers, out of the view of any cameras that might get a shot inside the courtroom through a window.

"All rise," yelled the bailiff, but the judge was already gone. The crowd burst to their feet asking questions as they fought forward. The new roar in the hall could be heard sweeping into the courtroom.

*"I'll have them call me when they're ready to release you, and I'll pick you up,"* Lar shouted over the noise to Marilyn.

She stood up and hugged him tight. "Thank you so much. I can't believe I'm finally free. The first thing I'm going to do is take a long, hot bath to get that stinking jail off me." As she said it, she watched Mr. and Mrs. Stonek over Lar's shoulder embrace.

*"I didn't do it,"* Lar said as they pulled apart. *"You did this."* But all three of them knew he'd closed the deal to make her trick work, at least to get her immediate release. Lar thought she'd done it anyway if Larry had prevailed and settled for her spending a few years in prison. A woman bailiff tugged at her elbow and led her back to the holding cell.

As he watched her leave, a voice coolly said behind him, "Congratulations." It was Simms. Reporters quickly opened their phones and started taking pictures as they shouted questions at the Stoneks leaving with their attorneys. The disturbed bailiffs shouted for the reporters to be quiet and close their phones or leave the courtroom.

*"Thanks,"* Lar said as he turned to face Simms, and they both watched the circus. Then Lar asked, *"Buy me a drink to celebrate? We're both so happy."*

"No, thanks, I'm headed to the gym, but I guess this simplifies my life," Simms said, watching some of the reporters chase the Stoneks out of the courtroom. Others turned and waited for Lar.

*"How's that?"* Lar asked as he stepped toward them and away from Simms.

"Now I can concentrate on Bain," Simms said to him as he walked away.

*"You do that,"* Lar said without turning around.

Simms put his hand on Lar's shoulder. "I appreciate you taking that test. Now that you're clear, we can really concentrate on finding the murderer, whoever you are."

Lar pulled away and stepped into the crowd of excited reporters.

# CHAPTER 18

Lar eased through the reporters like a shepherd walking through his flock. The crowd's hysteria, screamed questions, and camera flashes tasted like victory. None knew that the outcome had nothing to do with his legal brilliance, but just her coordinated manipulations.

Lacy's face appeared briefly in the anarchy. It was the first time Lar had seen him brave the ignorant masses. Lacy knew the truth, but he was irrelevant. Lar ebbed through the crowd, pretending that it was the flow of screamers halting him, but what he was really doing was giving each camera as much time as needed to fill its memory with photographs. He'd be so famous now—and Marilyn infamous—that they'd go anywhere as royalty.

But there was still his itch—Simms. He was there today—he's always there now—and he'd have much more time and incentive to investigate Brian's death. Lar heard what he said as Lar left the courtroom. Simms ruined Lar's victory parade when he played a card by saying, "Whoever you are." Simms knew. Somehow, Simms knew. There couldn't have been enough in the psychiatric records to tell Simms about him. There was just a diagnosis. But now, with that comment, he couldn't really enjoy his triumph because he had a gun to his head. He passed the test, but Simms's statement meant he knew the truth and how Lar beat it.

Lacy's face reappeared in the crowd, and they momentarily locked eyes. Lar twitched his head in friendly acknowledgment, and then he moved on—now picking up speed, not answering questions, not posing for pictures—toward the elevator, but he couldn't help himself; he couldn't resist, as usual. At the elevator door he turned to his audience, held up his hand dramatically, and said quietly to manipulate the loud reporters, *"I'll make a statement. I'll say something for you."*

The moving crowd alternated between screams for him to wait until their cameras were set up to shouts of silence so that they could hear Lar's whispers. He was encircled by a swirling cone of human arms and electronic devices, and he didn't wait. *"I'm happy today that justice was done. My client should have never been charged with a crime. A crime she was an innocent victim of, and I'm only sorry the truth of her true innocence can now never be told in public, in court, the same way her face and name have been constantly betrayed as guilty. I'm proud, very proud, to stand beside her."* That'll make them talk. Indiscernible questions were shouted, and he continued, *"I'll have more to say in the near future. I'll be available for individual interviews. Thank you."*

He turned and stepped into the next opened elevator, refusing to say more to the now insanely screaming reporters, and escaped as the door shut. A few jumped into the elevator with him, but he wouldn't answer their questions either. They'd have to book interviews with his office. Lar figured he could run his fame out years longer with interviews—hell, even a book. He just had to solve his one remaining problem, and he had to do it quickly.

Two hours later, he picked Marilyn up in the jail's basement garage, where the reporters couldn't follow. When the elevator door opened and a free, smiling Marilyn in civilian clothes stood there, he barely recognized her. He'd only seen her one other time out of her jail-issued orange overalls. She wore a cheap pantsuit, nothing Lar would've ever imagined her in, but she jumped in his car and hugged him like they'd not seen each other for six months. They'd never been alone, though he wanted them to both feel like this was the middle of their long-term relationship. They squeezed tight, and held onto each other until a car behind honked for them to get out of the way. They kissed again slowly before he put the car in gear and escaped the garage with nothing but videos of his dark-windowed Mercedes as he drove away.

"Where are we going? I need a bath, a hot bath, and new clothes. These hideous things are all I had at the jail."

*"Do you want me to take you by your place to get some clothes?"*

"It's gone. I was in jail so long that my rent got too far behind and the landlord sold everything." She looked at him as he drove, her eyes searching for his, and said, "I'm sorry. You're getting a girl with nothing."

Maybe. *"I wouldn't say that."*

"Are we going to your place?"

*"The Lux."*

Her smile grew. "A hotel."

*"You know I have a suite there."*

"Good. We have the rest of the afternoon and all night. Where are we going out to eat tonight?"

*"Can't. I've got an emergency I have to take care of. I thought I could make an appointment for this evening for you with an executive buyer, and you could go over there and buy some new clothes, shoes."*

"Oh." She betrayed a serious thought, then instantly returned to her exact same smile. "That sounds nice," she said as the car pulled in front of the hotel and a young valet rushed out to open her door, and then she asked knowingly, "And why are you getting rid of me?"

They both popped out of the car and passed into the lobby. As they walked, employees and guests stopped what they were doing and watched as the celebrities went by. As they rode the elevator, they couldn't talk because the other two riders, speechless, watched them like they were stars. Marilyn peeked at him and then their audience with a hidden smile only he saw. She enjoyed this as much as he did. They were two wolves in a world of sheep.

When the elevator opened on his floor and they stepped out and walked to the suite, she said nothing, waiting for him to answer her question. As she stepped into his room, she said, "Beautiful." It had a large modern kitchen to her left, with stainless steel appliances, and in front of her was an expansive den, with a large television hanging above a fireplace, leather furniture, and on the other side a roomy patio overlooking the city.

He shut the door and said, *"I have a little mess I have to clean up—that's all."*

Marilyn walked into the middle of the den, with every blind open and the sun shining on her back as she faced Lar, and she shed her clothes and pranced back to him. She put her arms around him, kissed him as he pressed on her lower back, and said, "That'll hold you until I get my hot bath." And then she slowly walked into his bedroom looking for the bathroom.

As she walked away, he thought as he watched her white, naked bottom that she'd lost weight in jail even since Larry first saw her, and he liked her performance, even here. She certainly knew how to handle him—any man, really. Lar calculated in his head the rest of the day and what time he had to be where. He called the department store six blocks away and made a reservation for a private stylist to meet Marilyn at five. He arranged a hotel car and driver for her. He made sure to let the concierge know he'd be in the suite while she was gone.

As he finished his work, Marilyn stepped out wrapped in a little white towel brushing her wet hair. She smiled, posed, and walked to him, and then dropped her towel and pressed her naked body against him while they kissed. She ripped his tie and shirt off, and they grabbed and jerked at each other all the way to the bed. They weren't drawing blood, but neither were they too careful not to hurt each other—more like two vicious dogs than lovers. When they finished, she called room service for a steak, rare, and then said, "What's your mess?"

He didn't pretend by asking her what she was talking about—she knew, and he knew she knew. He didn't answer her quickly enough, and she said, "It's Simms, isn't it? He thinks you did that guy...Bain."

Lar walked out to the den looking for nothing, just giving himself a second to think, and then he walked back to the bedroom, where she was sitting up in bed, naked, open, under the white sheet, smiling, and she said, "What's our plan?"

Bring her in? Why not? She's done it before, and while she's not that good at giving others complete instructions about how to finish a job right, she's good at lying, and that's all she had to do. Trust her? Not really, but he didn't need to trust her. It was totally in her interest that with Stonek back with his wife, her remaining sugar daddy stay free, and he wouldn't tell her anything else to give her any greater ability to blackmail him if she was so inclined—so bring her in.

As he took one of his guns from a drawer, he said, *"You just need to be with me here all night. Get home by eight, where I'm waiting for you watching television. After that, we're making love all night."*

"Um…"—she drew the word out—"I like that," she said in a way any normal person would fully believe she was being sexy and serious, but he knew she was uttering the mere words to provoke him into continuing his explanation, which he wouldn't do.

*"That's all. When I get home, we'll finish what we started."*

"I thought we did," she said as she crawled out from under the sheet and slowly walked to Lar so he could enjoy her body until she kissed him as she stroked the gun. "You're not going to tell me?" she whispered as she pecked-kissed him.

*"The less you know…"*

She wrapped her hands around the back of his neck and squeezed. "Are you protecting me?"

*"And you're protecting me."*

After Marilyn left, Lar guessed when Simms might have started his workout, and he slipped out of the back of the vacant service entrance of the hotel, remembering from past use it had no security cameras. He walked the two blocks on the street to avoid the cameras in the downtown tunnels and walkways to the health club's garage. He wished he had his car here for after, but he couldn't be seen leaving the hotel or parking on the street, so he'd have to slowly, anonymously, walk back the way he came, just like Razumihin. He dressed in dark clothing—runner's long pants, a pullover, a wide-brim cap—nothing special or noticeable. He leaned against a wall in a corner, almost disappearing into the wall, much like he bet Ava Stonek's third shooter probably did waiting on her. It made him laugh. If some idiot that Marilyn and Stonek found could get away after that shooting, he was sure he could.

There were very few cars in the downtown garage at this time of night, and the flickering fluorescent lighting was weak. It was dark. He checked for cameras, but didn't see any. He was sure they were there, but it didn't matter; he'd leave them nothing to identify him by. He kept his head down and pulled his cap lower in front nervously. Then he saw that windbag whistling as he approached—heading to his car.

Simms wore a runner's shirt and shorts that were pulled up just like his pants. No gun—it must be in the workout bag he carried, if he had it with him at all. He didn't see Lar, but walked past, and Lar followed quietly until Simms noticed and turned.

"Lamb." Simms didn't sound startled; he just said it like he observed a fact, just like he always did. Talk. Talk. Talk. He saw and knew everything, and he had to tell you about it. Lar pulled the .38 out of his pocket and pointed it at Simms. The damn gun had dug into his leg all the way from the hotel. He popped the safety off with his thumb. Simms remained unfazed, but turned square to face Lar. "Wow, you've really lost control, haven't you?"

"*I'm fine.*" Simms's calmness unsettled Lar. He thought he heard something in the distant corner of the garage, but when he peeked, it was nothing. Stay focused. "*You're a psychiatrist, too?*"

Simms acted like he wanted to put his bag down, but hesitated as he looked at the gun shake, and his face changed as he realized Lar might actually shoot him. "I know if you were OK that you wouldn't do this, and that you were sick when you killed Bain, too."

"*This isn't a cop show. You're not going to reveal the truth and save yourself.*" He thought, "*Pull it. Pull it. No.*"

"Don't. Save yourself. Don't let being sick ruin your whole life. Your wife's life. Your kids' lives."

"*I don't have a wife.*"

"Yeah, you do. And kids. They love you. She loves you. I've talked to her. She's come to me. We can save you, but you've got to get help, real help. You can't walk out on them, and you've got to get away from that poison of a woman. She'll kill you if you let her," Simms said as he searched behind Lar for something, anything, Lar thought, to help him. There was nothing, no one.

"*Pull it,*" he thought again.

"See, you're waiting. You know I'm right…"

The bullet burst into Simms's stomach, and then the trigger kept being pulled until it clicked empty. Simms wrenched back and forth with each hit, trying not to fall, like a bull elk surrounded by wolves, knowing once he's down, he's done. And then he was down, spread out like the drama queen he was, but very little blood. Where was all the blood?

Lar heard the explosion but felt nothing as his back burst and he crashed to the floor, his head bouncing on the concrete. He tried to open his eyes, and his eyelids popped as the blood glue that held them shut released. He'd found the blood he was looking for. He smelled gas and oil and dirt and vomit. He spat the blood out of his mouth as he tried to roll over, but he didn't have any muscles; he didn't feel like he even had a body. This wasn't real. It didn't feel real. What was going on?

Larry awoke as Larry, clear and free, and his thoughts drifted to Diane and Danny and Katie. He missed them so much. They were really all that ever mattered. How did they ever get so far away? How did he let himself ever get so far away from them?

She grabbed his shoulder and flipped him over. Through coated eyelashes his misting, fading eyes could see a black coat, a hat, a woman, Marilyn, standing over him, looking. She bent over, grabbed his face, squeezed it, and put her hand on his neck.

Larry wanted to ask her what she was doing, but he just lay there.

She knelt down and shoved something in or out of his pockets, and she said, "Sorry, but just like you said, I had a mess I had to clean up."

Larry thought of Diane and his babies, and then he quit thinking.

If you enjoyed "Murder for Me' the author would love to hear from you. Follow his blog at http://RussellLittleAuthor.com, post a review on Amazon and connect with the him on social media.